HANGAR 18

The Thriller
of the UFO Cover-Up

FOR YEARS, THE UNITED STATES GOV-
ERNMENT AND THE AIR FORCE HAVE
DENIED THAT UFOs EXIST. . . .

• Why, then, is there a military regulation threatening fine and imprisonment for revealing UFO
information?

• What about secret documents released by the
Freedom of Information Act that tell of UFO
encounters?

• How did the U.S. suddenly develop the technology to pull ahead of the Russians in the space
race? Was a sophisticated guidance system sal-
vaged from a crashed UFO?

IS THE GOVERNMENT CONCEALING IN-
FORMATION IT CONSIDERS TOO STAR-
TLING TO REVEAL TO THE AMERICAN
PUBLIC? HANGAR 18 TELLS THE FULL,
EXCITING, DRAMATIC STORY.

HANGAR 18

starring
Gary Collins
Robert Vaughn
James Hampton
Philip Abbott
Joseph Campanella
Pamela Bellwood
Tom Hallick
Steven Keats
William Schallert
and
Darren McGavin as Harry Forbes

Screenplay by Steven Thornley

Story by Tom Chapman & James L. Conway

Produced by
Charles E. Sellier, Jr.

Directed by
James L. Conway

HANGAR 18

Robert Weverka
and
Charles E. Sellier, Jr.

Based on the Screenplay by Steven Thornley

Story by Tom Chapman & James L. Conway

BANTAM BOOKS
TORONTO · NEW YORK · LONDON

HANGAR 18
A Bantam Book / September 1980

ISBN 0-553-14473-1

Published simultaneously in the United States and Canada

Bantam Books are published by Bantam Books, Inc. Its trade-
mark, consisting of the words "Bantam Books" and the por-
trayal of a bantam, is Registered in U.S. Patent and Trademark
Office and in other countries. Marca Registrada. Bantam
Books, Inc., 666 Fifth Avenue, New York, New York 10103.

PRINTED IN THE UNITED STATES OF AMERICA

0 9 8 7 6 5 4 3 2 1

Acknowledgements

The authors wish to express their grateful appreciation to Julie Mair for her extensive research assistance in the preparation of this book.

Preface

There is overwhelming evidence that the events upon which this book is based have actually occurred.

The Freedom of Information Act has been used in the past several years to uncover previously secret CIA and Department of Defense documents concerning national and international incidents of UFO activity.

Is it merely the fear of public panic that has kept the lid of government censorship on these events, or has information been discovered that could profoundly change our lives and affect our future?

This book is dedicated to the military personnel, NASA technicians, and private citizens who have courageously stepped forward to share their knowledge of these events. They believe, as we do, that the public has a right to know the truth—regardless of its implications.

THE AUTHORS

I

"We're reading you fine, now," the capsule communicator said from Mission Control. "How is it at your end?"

Lew Price, the shuttle pilot, smiled with relief. The static that had been crackling in his earphones for the past five minutes had finally disappeared—like a hammer no longer pounding on his head. "Loud and clear, Capcom," he answered.

"We've got a pile of weather sitting on us here in Houston," Capcom said. "But I don't think it'll give you any trouble coming down at the Cape. Right now, we've got a time of thirty hours, fifty-two and ten, Lew. How about you?"

Lew Price glanced at the digital clock in the center of the control panel. "Copy, Capcom."

"Steve, you want to go through a rundown while we've still got the time?" This time the voice came from Harry Forbes, the NASA Flight Director in Houston.

"Roger," Steve Bancroft, the shuttle commander said. He reached across and pulled the flight manual checklist from its clips and drew a pencil from the pocket of his pressure suit. "Main oxygen tanks now at thirty-seven percent. Secondary still at ninety-eight-point-four. . . Cabin pressure five-point-five PSI . . ."

The flight had been routine so far—a milk run. Aside from the usual buffeting from fuel tank "slosh" the launch from the Cape had been as smooth as silk.

1

At six hundred miles up, they had settled into orbit, and after a few minor adjustments for attitude and inclination, they had sailed silently along at nine thousand knots for more than thirty hours now.

For Lew Price and Steve Bancroft, this was their third orbital shuttle flight. It was not much different from the hundreds of hours they had spent sitting in the shuttle flight simulator in Houston a year ago. Except that the blue-black sky outside the six small windows was not real sky. And there were no "Dr. Frankenstein" instructors throwing horror problems at you. "You've got a massive pressure leak in the cockpit!" Or, "Control jets number one, two and three are not functioning, and you're beginning to tumble!" Or, "There's a fire in the cargo hold!"

Both Lew and Steve much preferred the real thing. Compared to the high pressure chaos of the simulator, an actual orbit flight was like cruising along an empty freeway on Sunday afternoon.

In appearance and temperament, Lew Price and Steve Bancroft were almost exact opposites. Bancroft was a tall lanky man with a ruddy complexion and a hard, chiseled face. He could easily have passed for a truck driver or a thirty-five-year-old Midwestern farmer instead of a man with a Masters degree in engineering from Cal Tech. Price, a former navy jet pilot, was two years younger and three inches shorter, with a round face and an easy sense of humor that suggested there weren't a whole lot of things in the world he worried about.

"Okay, Steve," Capcom said from Mission Control. "Now, how about that number four computer? Are you still getting a red light?"

Bancroft put away the manual and punched some buttons on the control panel above his head. A red light at the side blinked off for a moment, then came back on. "It's intermittent, Capcom. It seems to have a little indigestion, or something."

"Roger. Same here," Harry Forbes said. "Try switching to the backup, Steve."

"Roger, flight." Bancroft pulled the switch-over lever and the red light went off. On the read-out screen, two sets of digital numbers came on, both clicking smoothly.

"That did it," Capcom said. "You're looking good, Steve."

"We always look good," Bancroft said.

Lew Price glanced at the computer and smiled slyly. "Hey, you guys . . ."

"Yes, Lew?"

"I know the NASA budget is tight, but I think you'd better quit buying those mail order kits for the electronics in this thing."

Normally, the joke would have brought laughter and some catcalls from the technicians at Mission Control. This time only a few restrained chuckles came through the earphones. Both Price and Bancroft knew why. Lt. General Frank Morrison of the Air Force— old spit and polish himself—was probably standing at the back of the room scowling at everybody down there.

General Morrison really wasn't so old. But this particular shuttle flight was on behalf of the Air Force. In the big cargo bay just behind the cockpit, they were carrying a twelve-hundred-pound satellite that would be launched into a twenty-five thousand mile orbit in a few minutes. For General Morrison, the satellite was serious business, and off and on through the last thirty-one hours it was always evident when he was present in the big Mission Control theatre. The jokes were kept to a minimum during those times.

"You're coming up on fourteen minutes to launch," Capcom said quietly.

"You'd better open the cargo bay doors, Colonel," the Payload Officer added.

Colonel Gates, a quiet man in his early forties, was manning the aft controls of the shuttle. Like General Morrison, Gates was Air Force, and took his work seriously. "Roger, Mission Control," he said and touched the "Unlock" button. "Cargo bay locks disengaged."

"Green light here," Payload affirmed.

The colonel pressed the "Open" button and a faint groan vibrated through the shuttle as the big sixty-foot-long doors separated at the top of the ship and opened outward. Five seconds later a soft clunk indicated the doors were spread wide exposing the entire mid-section of the ship. Gates rose partially from his seat and peered through the aft window that gave visual access to the cargo bay. "Bay doors open and in place," he said.

"Roger," Payload acknowledged.

Before the satellite rockets were fired, a big manipulator arm in the cargo bay would reach back and lift the satellite from the bay deck and hoist it a hundred feet up and off to the side of the shuttle. Activating the manipulator arm would be the next step.

"Twelve minutes to launch," Capcom announced.

"Colonel," Payload suddenly said, "we're getting a red light from the satellite. How about you?"

"Roger," Gates answered, "I'm getting it here, too."

Price and Bancroft were both twisted in their couch-chairs, watching the colonel. Price glanced at Bancroft and raised his eyebrows, half smiling. The Air Force people, including Colonel Gates, had been very insistent about double checking all the shuttle instruments and systems both before and after the lift off. But the satellite had been strictly their baby, with no NASA people allowed to go near it. Now, after all they had gone through to get the thing up to their six hundred mile orbit, it would be ironic if it didn't even work.

Gates was pushing buttons and pulling switches on a control panel the Air Force had installed specially for the flight. He paused for a minute, then tried them again. "Looks like a malfunction in a com module," he said.

"Right," the Payload Officer answered.

Gates tried the buttons again, glancing from the control panel to the window overlooking the cargo bay. "It's no go," he finally said. He gave it up and started unbuckling his harnesses. "Payload, I'm going to go out and have a look."

Capcom's voice came through with a warning tone. "You're coming up on ten minutes to launch."

Harry Forbes, the Flight Director, suddenly came on. "You want to hold the countdown?"

There was no doubt who answered the question. It was the commanding voice of General Morrison. "No," he said flatly. "That satellite has to launch on schedule."

Steve Bancroft groaned inwardly and turned back to glance at the flight instruments. The military mind at work, he reflected. Whether the satellite functioned or not, it had to be sent into orbit. Which meant they would accomplish nothing more than adding another piece of space junk to the earth's orbit.

Gates was moving toward the hatch that led to the lower deck. Lew Price quickly slipped out of his harnesses and moved to help him. In the airlock below, Gates would have to attach an umbilical tether before he went space walking out to the cargo bay. "You want some help?" Price asked.

Gates shook his head. "I can handle it," he said sharply, and lowered himself through the hatch.

Price shrugged and looked at Bancroft. "What's the matter with him?"

Bancroft smiled and touched a finger to his lips. "Secrets, secrets. I think he's got you pegged for a Russian spy."

Bancroft unbuckled his harness and joined Price at the window overlooking the cargo bay. The satellite was resting on a pallet that was secured to the deck by hydraulic clamps. It wasn't much different from a dozen other satellites Price and Bancroft had seen. It looked like a huge oil barrel with two rectangular wings that would spring into position when it reached its orbit altitude.

"What do you suppose it's gonna do?" Price asked.

Bancroft laughed. "Probably flush all the toilets in Moscow."

Their earphones crackled and Harry Forbes' voice came on. "What're you guys doing up there?"

"Colonel Gates is in the airlock chamber," Price answered. "I think he's looking for a parachute."

Capcom's voice interrupted in a flat monotone: "Eight minutes."

Gates finally appeared on the cargo deck below them. He steadied himself, then picked his way toward the satellite, checking his tether lines all the way, being careful not to snag them. He seemed to know what he was doing. He moved to the base of the big oil drum, drew a wrench from his pocket and quickly loosened four bolts.

"Seven minutes," Capcom's voice said.

Gates pulled off the panel. He secured it under his foot so it wouldn't drift away, then slid out an instrument tray. He curled forward, touching parts, studying them closely. He detached something, looked it over, then pressed it firmly back in place.

"What have you got, Colonel?" Forbes asked.

"A loose module," Gates answered.

Bancroft looked at the aft control panel. The red light had gone off and a pattern of numbers now flickered steadily across a green-faced monitor. "We're getting an affirmative reading here."

"Here, too," the Payload Officer answered.

"Good work, Colonel," Forbes said.

"Six minutes," Capcom's voice announced.

Gates lifted the control panel back into position and worked hurriedly at the bolts. Price smiled. "Simple," he said, then sang softly: "Nothing can stop the Army Air Force."

"Can we start lifting it?" Payload asked.

6

"Roger," Bancroft answered. He eased into Gates' chair and switched on the manipulator-arm controls. Out on the cargo bay, the arm consisted of three jointed shafts that would unfold to a length of slightly less than a hundred feet. A television camera was mounted on one of the arms, enabling the whole thing to be accurately maneuvered by remote control from inside the shuttle.

"Four minutes," Capcom said.

Price watched through the window as the hooked end of the manipulator arm rose snake-like from its berth. The larger joint opened, lifting the hooks eight feet into the air, and Bancroft skillfully maneuvered them toward the satellite. Colonel Gates had finished securing the panel bolts and was waiting to attach the hooks.

It was only by chance that Price glanced at the radar screen. He had stepped back from the aft window and gazed at Bancroft's TV monitor for a moment. Then he glanced at the other instruments and started to move back to the window. But the radar screen stopped him cold.

"What the . . . ?!"

Bancroft was concentrating hard on his TV monitor. "What's the matter?"

It had happened so quickly, Price was not certain what he had seen—or if he had seen anything at all. It seemed as if a blip had raced diagonally across the upper part of the radar screen, from left to right. But it had gone by so fast it seemed impossible. "Something traveling like a bat outa hell," he said. "Either that, or I blinked at the wrong time."

Bancroft lifted his head and glanced over. Almost at the same instant, the blip crossed again—this time traveling from right to left, tracing the same pattern in the opposite direction. It couldn't have taken more than a tenth of a second.

"There it is again!"

Bancroft frowned. "A meteor?"

7

"Not unless it made a U-turn," Price answered.

"Bancroft," Colonel Gates called from the cargo bay, "can you get the hooks over here? I need about three more feet, and a little to the right."

Bancroft turned back to the manipulator controls. Price frowned and kept his eyes on the radar screen, almost afraid to blink now. For something to have crossed the screen that fast, it had to have been traveling three or four hundred thousand miles an hour. Maybe faster. Two meteors going in opposite directions? It didn't seem likely. And the chance of their tracing the exact same pattern were one in a billion.

"Okay, that's it," Gates said from the cargo deck. "Give me a minute to hook it up."

"Flight . . . ?" Price said into his microphone.

"Roger," Forbes answered. "We're listening, Lew."

Price kept his eyes on the radar screen. "Harry . . . we're picking up something pretty wild on radar. You got anything down there?"

Harry Forbes' question was directed to the side. "Bob?" he asked.

Bob Reynolds, the Flight Activity Officer, answered: "We see it."

"What is it?"

"Beats me," Reynolds answered. "It's crossed twice now, but it's so damned fast . . ."

General Morrison's voice came in from the background. "Check Norad," he commanded someone.

"Okay," Colonel Gates said from the cargo deck. "We're hooked up. All the clamps are freed. Take it away."

Price looked over at Bancroft's TV monitor screen. The satellite was rising out of the bay, the manipulator arms slowly beginning to open out to their full length.

"One minute fifty seconds," Capcom's voice announced.

"Lew," Harry Forbes said at almost the same time, "we've just talked to Norad. They've picked up something too, and they're trying to get a fix on the speed. They say it's moving fast. Very fast."

"Roger," Price answered. He watched the satellite rise another ten feet, then turned his attention back to the radar screen. It was solid green now; not a flicker of white. Whatever had roared past them might be halfway to the moon by this time.

Price was about to turn away when the blip appeared again. This time it crossed the top of the screen and disappeared, traveling at less than half its former speed. "Steve!" he exclaimed, then caught his breath. The blip was in the screen again, now traveling more slowly than ever.

"One minute to launch," Capcom's voice droned.

The blip angled down from the left corner, moving directly at them. Then, like a stalking cat making its final leap, the thing darted quickly to the center of the screen and stopped dead.

"My God," Price gasped, "according to this, it's directly *above* us!"

Bancroft was gaping at the radar screen, his hands suddenly motionless on the manipulator controls. "What the . . . ?"

Price moved quickly to the window. The glare of harsh sunlight blinded him as he looked up. With his hand, he blocked it out as best he could, then squinted, pressing his cheek to the heavy glass. "Holy Christ . . . something's up there! It's right above us!"

Bancroft was behind him, trying to squeeze into position to see. But neither of them could see any more than a small segment of whatever it was. The intense glare of the sun was flashing off the side, blotting out all but the fuzzy outlines of a curving edge. Nor could they tell how far away it was. Then it moved, easing slowly out of their line of vision.

"Thirty seconds to launch," Capcom said.

Price and Bancroft moved quickly to the forward

windows, leaning as close as possible to see upward. From there the sun was worse. It hit them squarely in the eyes, making it impossible to focus on the object. Again they could see nothing more than a blurred edge.

"What is it?" Bancroft cried. The white light beneath the object seemed almost as bright as the sun behind it.

Capcom's voice came through, starting the final countdown, apparently oblivious to the intruder. "Ten seconds . . . nine . . . eight . . ."

Bancroft pulled away from the forward controls and crossed to the aft window. "Gates!" he called out, "do you see it?!"

The Air Force colonel was standing in the center of the cargo deck, one hand gripping the empty satellite cradle, the other shading his eyes, as he squinted upward. His mouth was open, an incredulous look on his face. He nodded, his voice half choked. "Yes . . . I see it."

Capcom's voice continued the countdown: "Five . . . four . . ."

"Steve?" Harry Forbes voice called through the speaker, "Lew . . . ?"

"Two . . . one . . . ignition!"

Price and Bancroft both saw it happen. There was a quick burst of rocket fire, and the satellite jumped instantly from the end of the manipulator arm. As quickly as it was gone there was a thunderous explosion; a huge ball of flame blossoming less than two hundred feet above them. Liquid fire spewed out in all directions. Then more flames and bits of debris from the disintegrating satellite whirled past in a shower of sizzling fire.

"My God!" Price breathed. The sight was horrifying. Still he couldn't take his eyes from it. The object—whatever it was—must have been completely enveloped in the satellite's rocket fuel. The flames were still dancing wildly around it, sending more pieces of satellite debris sputtering off into space. Inside Price's helmet, his earphones were filled with a deafening roar of static.

Why didn't the object move? he wondered. The flames were swirling in a convulsive, self-consuming fireball, with the object somewhere in the center of it! Then, as if responding to his question, it seemed to slide away, dropping off to the starboard side of the shuttle. The flames were dying, but the sun glinting off the object's surface still made it impossible to see.

It was moving toward earth now, steadily gaining speed. An instant later it was a tiny disc, then an almost invisible speck. The radio static also diminished; then Harry Forbes' urgent voice was coming through.

"Come in, Orbiter, come in! Steve . . . Lew . . . can you hear me?!"

Price looked across the cockpit at Bancroft, neither of them able to speak for a moment.

"Steve . . . Lew . . . do you read me?!" Forbes shouted.

Bancroft nodded. "Yeah," he said hoarsely, "we hear you, Harry."

General Morrison's angry voice suddenly broke in. "What happened up there?"

The Payload Officer's voice came on before they could answer. "The satellite exploded!" he exclaimed.

Pieces of satellite debris were still bouncing off the shuttle, spinning away as if in slow motion. Price moved quickly to the forward window and peered upward. There was still a cloud of debris around them, from chunks of twisted metal to tiny specks of reflecting material.

"Steve . . . Lew?" Forbes' voice called, "do you read me?"

"Yeah," Bancroft answered from a side window.

"What happened?"

"Whatever that thing was," Bancroft answered, "the satellite hit it and . . ."

Reynolds, the Flight Activity Officer, broke in:

"We've lost our medical readings on Gates. Is he all right, Steve?"

Bancroft turned quickly to the aft window, pressing his face close, trying to see directly below, among the pieces of debris floating in the cargo bay. Gates was nowhere in sight.

"Steve!" Price suddenly exclaimed from the front window. He was pointing downward and slightly off to the port side. Bancroft moved quickly to the side window. "Good Lord," he breathed.

Gates was floating past them, tilted at a crazy angle, one knee bent, the other leg stretched out to the side. Both his hands were grasping the severed four-foot length of his umbilical tether. His helmet was four feet away, floating along at the same speed. His mouth was open, his face a rigid mask of agony.

There was no possibility of his still being alive. Without oxygen and pressure for his suit the vacuum of space would have immediately exhausted his lungs of air.

"Harry?" Bancroft said thickly.

"What is it, Steve?"

"Gates. We . . . we've lost him. He's dead."

Bancroft knew his words echoed through Mission Control, stabbing into every man there. Probably very few of them knew Colonel Gates. But his presence on a shuttle mission made him a brother to all of them. On space flights, everybody was everyone else's keeper. Bancroft could hear the quiet groans and the soft oaths. Harry Forbes' voice finally came through, heavy, burdened with shock.

"What happened, Steve?"

Bancroft took a deep breath, his eyes still on Gates' slowly drifting body. "He must have been hit by the debris. From the satellite."

"The umbilical was severed," Price added quietly. "His helmet was ripped off."

"Can you get him, Steve? The body, I mean?"

Bancroft nodded. "Yes, we'll get him."

Both men moved quietly to their chairs and buckled in. Price activated the control jets, and within moments they were sliding forward, gradually overtaking Gates' body. Then, handling the controls with expert delicacy, he maneuvered the ship until Gates' body was floating at the side, almost touching the open cargo door.

It took Bancroft three minutes to go below, attach an umbilical tether and bring Gates' body back. In the air lock, he stretched out the body and covered it, all in silence from Mission Control. When he returned to the cockpit, he reported that Gates was secure.

"Okay," Forbes' voice said with a heavy sigh, "let's get back to work, everybody. We've still got two men up there. Shuttle, we have twenty seconds to loss of signal. We'll start re-entry sequence over the Indian Ocean station. Copy?"

"Copy," Bancroft said softly.

The twenty seconds passed in silence, then Bancroft switched off the radio. He looked at Price, who was staring vacantly out the window. "It's a lousy way to die," he said.

"Yeah," Price nodded. "What do you suppose that thing was?"

Bancroft shook his head. "I don't know what to think. My God . . . going that fast . . . making those kinds of maneuvers . . . it certainly wasn't any kind of spacecraft we know of."

"Russian, possibly?"

Bancroft considered the question. "It would be hard to believe they're that far ahead of us."

"You know," Price said, still shaken by the experience, "I never believed any of those saucer stories. I've been flying a long time, and I've never seen anything even remotely resembling a UFO." He snorted softly. "Even if I did, I'm not sure I would have reported it."

"Well, you won't have to report this one. They've got it all on tapes in Houston."

13

II

The atmosphere at Mission Control was funereal. The joking and the easy smiles were gone, and those who had business were talking in hushed voices and moving around the big room almost on tiptoes.

Harry Forbes sat quietly in the middle of it, his eyes fixed vacantly on the big screen that showed the minute-by-minute progress of the shuttle as it made its sine-wave curves around the earth. He was a rumpled man in his mid-forties, wearing an open shirt and a light sweater. In one capacity or another, he had been at the job for nineteen years now. But this had been the first time anybody had even come close to having a serious accident while they were in space.

That the man had been an Air Force officer instead of a NASA man made it even worse. Maybe he should have countermanded General Morrison's order and stopped the countdown. Maybe he should have insisted they wait until Gates was back in the cockpit, or in the air lock before they fired the satellite rockets.

"Harry?"

Phil Cameron came up beside him and leaned an arm on the console, a questioning look on his face. Cameron was a thirty-four-year-old aeronautical engineer, and had been Harry's right-hand man for the past six years. "I've run the tapes back to where the blips showed up on the radar screen," he said. "You want to look at them?"

Harry nodded and reluctantly pulled himself from

the chair. He followed Cameron across the room to a tape machine standing near the wall.

"The first one comes about three minutes and forty seconds before the satellite launch," Cameron said. He rolled the tape, and Harry watched the screen and the digital clock counter at the top. At the exact time, a white spot raced across the top of the screen so fast it was barely visible. The second one came about eight seconds later, crossing in the opposite direction.

"And then, . . ." Cameron said and pushed the tape into fast-forward, ". . . about fifty seconds before launch, this." He switched the tape to normal speed and they watched as the blip made a slower pass across the screen. A moment later it returned and edged close to the shuttle, finally darting into the center of the screen.

"Now the satellite rockets are fired," Cameron said.

The blip seemed to bulge for an instant. Then tiny pieces flew away in all directions. Moments later, the blip moved slowly off to the side of the screen and finally disappeared.

"Has General Morrison seen this?" Harry asked.

"Not yet."

Harry glanced around the room. "Where is he?"

Phil Cameron nodded toward the glassed-in offices at the back. Morrison was in an office, standing close to the window, a phone at his ear. By the grim expression on his face, he didn't look like he wanted to be disturbed.

"When he comes out, tell him you've got the tapes," Harry said. "And Phil, you'd better contact the Cape and tell them to have an ambulance standing by when the shuttle comes down."

"Right."

Forbes returned to his chair and watched the big tracking screen for another minute, wondering about that blip. There was no question about there having been something up there—something that moved very fast, and was extremely maneuverable. There also seemed to be no doubt that it hovered over the shuttle, and that the satellite crashed into it at almost the same instant it launched. So what the hell was it, and where had it come from? And maybe more important, where had it gone after it eased away from the shuttle?

Sam Tate emptied the last half-inch of beer from the can and banged the empty down on the zinc bar. But it was so noisy in the place nobody heard it. Behind him, the juke box was blasting out a country tune so loud you could probably hear it all the way across the Arizona border into New Mexico. And along the bar and at the tables, everybody was trying to talk loud enough to be heard over the music.

"Hey, Pete!" Sam called out in a thick voice. He had been drinking since supper time, and the old clock with the Schlitz neon sign around it said a quarter to one.

Pete Lakakis, the owner and sole bartender in Pete's Polish Palace, took his foot off the cooler where he was talking to three cowboys at the other end of the bar and came smiling down. "What can I do for you, Sam?"

"Gimme another beer, huh?" Sam fumbled his wallet from a back pocket of his frayed jeans and found a wrinkled five-dollar bill in the bottom. He squinted hard at the battered old wallet, a little surprised there was no more than the single bill in it.

"You sure you want any more, Sam?" Pete asked.

It took a moment for Sam to figure out what the question meant. Then he grinned and pushed the bill across the bar. "Aw hell, I ain't gonna drink it now. I'm just gonna take it with me and have it for breakfast tomorrow. A little hair for the dog, you know? In fact, why don't you give me a couple of 'em."

Pete pulled two cans of Pearl out of the cooler and set them on the bar. He rang the sale up on the cash register and gave Sam his change. "You take care driving home now, Sam."

"Don't you worry none about me," Sam grinned. He shoved a can into each of the pockets of his sheepskin jacket and moved unsteadily for the door. "See y'all tomorra," he called out, and lumbered through the door.

It was cold out. He stood by the front door for a minute, looking up at the bright moonlit sky, then found the way to his car. The car was a rusting twenty-year-old Ford he had bought in Phoenix six months ago for eighty dollars. He had to slam the door three times before it finally caught. Then he popped open one of the beer cans and downed half of it in one long gurgle. Damn, he thought. Payday was still three days off, and he had only about four dollars left. He had been working out at Mr. Keller's place, taking care of his horses for the last couple of weeks. But he doubted if Mr. Keller would look too kindly on his asking for an advance on his salary. He finished the beer, tossed the can into the back seat and got the engine running. Okay now, he told himself. He had to be careful driving. He had to watch out for those damned kids screaming around in their pickup trucks. He backed the car out, swung across the gravel and looked both ways before he pulled onto the highway.

For the past month or so he had been living in a run-down trailer court about six miles down the road. But he was going to get out of there pretty quick. Maybe when he got his next pay check he could drive down to Tucson and see what was going on. A couple years ago he had had a good job there. It was driving a truck and sloshing out the stables for a man named Peters. The pay wasn't that much. But they gave him a nice little shed to stay in. Had a kitchen and everything.

Holding the steering wheel straight with his leg, he popped open the other beer can and took a big gulp, then sang, "I once had a girl, and her name was . . ."

Sam's mouth suddenly came open and he gaped through the windshield. Then he grabbed the steering wheel with both hands and jammed his foot on the brake pedal, slopping beer over the dashboard as the car skidded to a stop.

He didn't pay any attention to the spilled beer. Off to his right an airplane was streaking toward the ground in what looked like a long, sharp dive. From the bright, blinking lights, it looked like a big one, maybe a jumbo jet. Sam held his breath as it seemed to level out a little. But it wasn't going to make it. It was going much too fast to pull out. It was streaking in front of him now, crossing the highway three or four miles ahead of him, angling down toward a hill about a mile short of the mountains.

Then it was gone behind the hill, and Sam stared, waiting, expecting some kind of an explosion, or a burst of flames to light up the sky behind the hill. But nothing happened. There was no sound, and no sign of flames. "Holy Jesus!" he said softly. The thing had crashed—there was no doubt about that. Was it out of fuel, maybe, and didn't catch fire?

There was a dirt road going out in that direction. Sam remembered going by it dozens of times. He took another big swallow of beer, set the can on the seat beside him and headed down the highway, watching closely. Still, there were no flames or any sign of fire. When he saw the road, he swung off the highway and gunned the engine. The tires squealed off the pavement, and then he was bouncing and sliding at forty miles an hour up the dirt road.

The road went on the wrong side of the hill. But it was rising, going up toward a little saddle on the far side. Sam held the throttle down, taking quick glances at the hill as he climbed steadily higher.

It came suddenly, just as he reached the high ground of the saddle. He saw a dozen or more lights in a straight, horizontal line, all of them blinking on and off together. He hit the brakes again, sliding to a stop, not quite believing his eyes.

The thing was about fifty yards down the other side of the hill, sitting in an almost level area. Sam stared at it, breathing heavily now, all kinds of crazy thoughts running through his head. It couldn't be an airplane. If it was, it would have been smashed to pieces the way it came down. And it wasn't even the right shape. It looked like it was resting on some kind of a rounded platform, about forty or fifty feet long. The blinking lights were all around the edges of the platform, and above that there seemed to be big black humps—three, maybe four of them—all crowded together and standing about eighteen or twenty feet high.

Sam knew what it was. He knew, and his pounding heart seemed to be pushing up into his throat as he stared at it. *Holy Jesus!* he thought. It was some kind of UFO . . . or flying saucer . . . and inside of it there had to be some kind of living things to make it operate.

Sam looked wildly out the windows on both sides of the car. There was enough room to turn around. The area was flat, and the dirt was packed. He turned the steering wheel hard to the right and swung the car into the brush. Then he quickly backed up until he was on the road again and facing in the opposite direction. He gave the thing one final look as he shoved the accelerator down, and the car whipped and slithered down the hill.

Captain James Wyatt leaned far forward in his seat and squinted hard at the rocky desert terrain three hundred feet below. The pilot had lifted the big Huey chopper over a high ridge and swooped into a narrow valley that was strewn with giant boulders and gouged by flashflooding. They were moving south along the east perimeter now, all four of the crew members searching the ground below, looking for anything that might qualify as a grounded unidentified flying object.

The order to scramble had come thirty-five minutes earlier. Wyatt had been in bed and sleeping soundly when the telephone rang and he found himself talking to General Becker, the base commander.

"Captain, you're not going to believe this," the general said quietly, "but there's some kind of unidentified spacecraft down about twenty miles southeast of here. I just got a call from General Morrison in Houston. He wants us to find it as fast as possible."

"You mean a . . . a flying saucer, or something?"

The general had hesitated. "Let's just say an unidentified spacecraft."

"Yes, sir." By then Wyatt had his pants on and was pulling on his boots, the phone cradled to his shoulder.

"Apparently Norad tracked its descent," General Becker went on. "They've got a good fix on the spot where it landed. I've already sent the coordinates out to the pad with Lt. Brock. And, Captain . . ."

"Yes, sir?"

"This is to be kept top secret. That's by order of General Morrison."

"I understand, sir."

"And if you find anything, General Morrison wants to know immediately. He wants us to patch your radio directly to Houston."

Wyatt had been the last one to reach the pad. The helicopter rotors were already turning, and the moment he vaulted into the cargo bay they were lifting off and swinging to the southeast.

The coordinates Norad had given them were down to plus-or-minus three navigational minutes. But in these latitudes, that meant an area of about thirty-six square miles. And in terrain that was folded and scarred with ridges and desert washes, it was hard to make distinctions between clumps of bushes and dark outcroppings of rock.

The moon didn't help. Hanging low in the west, it

cast long shadows from boulders, and turned the ravines into black, bottomless trenches. Several times they had altered their course to investigate what appeared to be perfectly symmetrical circles, or glints of reflected light from shiny objects. But the helicopter's big searchlights turned them into patches of brush, or ancient dump sites with piles of broken bottles.

"You want to go back up the other side of the valley, Captain?" the pilot shouted over the sputtering roar of the engines.

Wyatt shook his head and pointed south. "Try the other side of the ridge."

The pilot nodded and swung the helicopter south, lifting it another two hundred feet to clear the jagged wall of rock. On the other side, the slopes ran down into flat desert. To the east there was a small hill with what appeared to be a dirt road running around the near side. The road curved downward and ran a couple of miles south to a highway. Wyatt motioned toward the hill.

The pilot dropped down to two hundred feet, skirting the edge of the slopes, keeping the nose tilted forward. Then he rose another hundred feet as they approached the hill. Wyatt scanned the terrain below, seeing nothing more than brush and sand. They skimmed over the saddle connecting the hill with the higher terrain, and then Wyatt caught his breath as he stared out the side window. "Hold it!" he shouted. "Over there!"

The pilot couldn't see it from his position in the cockpit. He swung the ship to the right, then tilted it, making a broad circle.

"Holy shit!" he said.

The thing was about forty feet across, what looked like a black mass of steel, surrounded by thirty or forty blinking amber lights.

"What the hell is it?" the pilot yelled.

Wyatt was too stunned to answer. It wasn't until now, he realized, that he really hadn't expected to find anything out here. With all the thousands of UFO sightings, he had never heard of any government officials or military people coming across one. At least they had never reported one sitting on the ground anywhere.

Lt. Brock came bursting into the cockpit. "Jesus, Captain, did you see that damned thing?!"

Wyatt continued to stare at the thing, then grabbed the microphone, suddenly aware that his heart was pounding wildly. "C Base Seven, this is Bravo Two. Over."

The speaker crackled for an instant, then: "C Base Seven. Go ahead, Captain."

"Can you patch me through to General Morrison in Houston? He's expecting me."

"It's already done, Captain. Hold on."

The pilot had eased the helicopter fifty yards to the side of the object and eased down to twenty or thirty feet. Wyatt stared at the thing until the general came on.

"Morrison," the voice said flatly.

"General, this is Captain Wyatt out of C Base Seven. We have located the spacecraft. We're hovering about fifty yards from it right now." Wyatt didn't know what more to say. The helicopter pilot had risen half out of his seat and was leaning over him to get a better view.

The general was silent for a moment—as stunned as they were, maybe. "What kind of a craft is it, Captain?" he finally asked.

Wyatt shook his head. "I don't know, General."

The general's voice came back with a sharp edge. "Well, what can you see?"

"Lights," Wyatt said. "Blinking lights. Around the base of it."

"And . . . ?"

Wyatt finally realized he wasn't being much help. But what could he say about something he had never seen before? "Sir, it's about forty feet across . . . a little longer than it is wide . . . with rounded ends. Fifteen or twenty feet high. Black in color. Shiny black. It's like it's sitting on a platform, sir. The lights are all around the platform, and . . . and the upper part . . . some kind of superstructure . . . four or five humped modules all grouped together."

"No sign of life around it?"

"No, sir. At least not on the outside."

Again the general paused, apparently thinking, trying to digest the information. "All right, Wyatt, I want you to keep your position. Don't leave there, and don't use your radio until you hear from me. Understand?"

"Yes, sir."

"I'll call you back within fifteen minutes."

The radio clicked off before Wyatt had a chance to answer. He put the mike back on its hook and stared once more at the shadowy object. From somewhere behind the cockpit one of the other men had turned on a second spotlight. He was slowly playing it back and forth across the craft. Whoever, or whatever, was inside the thing seemed oblivious to the fact that they were being watched. The lights continued to pulse—like some kind of automated neon sign outside a cheap diner.

Jesus, Wyatt thought, what the hell should they do if a door opened and something or somebody came out of the thing? He took a deep, steadying breath, hoping he wouldn't have to answer that question.

III

Price and Bancroft went through their systems and instruments check-out procedures with more than usual care as they approached the re-entry countdown. There was no more bantering with the technicians in Houston, and the voices from below were equally businesslike.

"Okay, Steve," Harry Forbes finally said. "You want to pull the manipulator arm back in and close the bay doors?"

"Roger," Bancroft answered and made his way to the aft controls.

The arm came down smoothly, folding itself into its berth with a soft *clunk*. "Arm in place and secure," Bancroft reported. He pressed the "bay door closure" button, expecting to hear the soft hiss of hydraulics and see the window above the control panel go dark. The sound came. Five seconds later there was the soft *clunk* of a door fitting into place. But the aft window was not dark, and a red light came on, indicating "no function" on the starboard side. Bancroft tried the button again, then switched to the back-up system. Still no reaction.

"We're getting a negative function on the starboard door," Harry Forbes said from Houston.

"Roger," Bancroft affirmed. He quickly rose and pressed his helmet against the window. The starboard door was still extended horizontally from the side of the ship; it hadn't moved an inch. "Damn," he said quietly. Still watching through the window, he pressed the button again. The big sixty-foot-long door vibrated. The forward edge moved upward several inches as if struggling to close. But the rear section remained locked in place. "No go, Harry."

Lew Price was twisted in his seat, watching. "They don't close . . . we don't go home."

There would be stability problems with re-entry into the atmosphere, but there was a chance they could make it. After that it would be highly doubtful. Maneuvering the ship into a two-hundred-mile-an-hour landing on three miles of concrete was tricky as it was. Doing it with an extra pair of wings that were not designed for aerodynamics was highly questionable.

"Harry?" Bancroft said. "We were hit by a lot of junk when that satellite exploded. I'm going to go out and take a look."

The all too recent memory of Colonel Gates' walk in the cargo bay gave Forbes' voice an uneasy note. "Okay, Steve. Be careful."

Lew Price moved to the aft controls as Bancroft dropped through the hatch into the air lock. Two minutes later, Bancroft emerged on the cargo deck, half floating, pulling his way past the empty satellite pallet. He picked up a piece of jagged metal and gave it a toss, sending it flying off into space. Then he moved back to the corner where the cargo door was joined to the ship. He moved forward again, studying the hinged edge of the door. Then he stopped abruptly.

"See anything, Steve?" Price asked. Bancroft was hunched over one of the hinges, his shoulders working. "Steve?"

He was smiling when he finally straightened from the hinge. "I think I've found our problem." He lifted what looked like a fragment of flattened pipe. "Jammed into the hinge," he said. "See if you can close it, Lew. Slow and easy."

Price let out a sigh of relief and touched the "closure" button. The soft hissing was the prettiest music he had heard in days. The door rose steadily, arching over the cargo bay. Then it clunked softly into place. The window was dark now. "Closed and locked," he said into his microphone.

"Roger," Harry said.

Price could hear the sighs of relief at Mission Control. Two minutes later Bancroft was coming through the hatch, still carrying the piece of metal. He gave Price a rueful smile and tucked the metal away where it wouldn't bounce around the cockpit.

"Harry," Price said solemnly into his mike, "I think I'd kinda like to come home now."

"Roger," Forbes answered. "Is Steve there?"

"I'm here and ready," Bancroft answered, replugging his pressure suit.

"Okay, you're still on schedule. We've got about two and a half minutes. You want to start rotation?"

"Commencing rotation," Price answered as they both tightened their harnesses.

Along with the first few moments of launch, re-entry was always a ticklish time that sent the heart creeping toward the throat. After what they had been through in the last few hours, it seemed like a piece of cake this time. The shuttle was rotated into its backward-flying position, the entry angle was adjusted to six and a half degrees, and the burn and the buffeting and the deafening roar began with more a feeling of relief than uneasiness.

At Mission Control, Harry Forbes experienced the same relief. The heat was normal, the angle was perfect, and all flight instruments showed they would be on target for descent. He eased back in his chair, then glanced across the room as he saw General Morrison striding toward him from the offices. The general was still wearing his grim face, as if his troubles had deepened in the past hour and a half.

Forbes couldn't blame him. The mission had been a failure. Whatever the satellite was supposed to do up there, the job would have to be put off for at least another month, maybe longer. He had also lost a man in the disaster.

"Forbes," the general said when he reached Harry's station, "I want to talk to you." He glanced at the nearby technicians, then lowered his voice and gestured toward the offices. "Now," he added.

It was a command rather than a request. Forbes stared at him, then removed his headset and rose. "Phil?" he said to Cameron. "Take over, will you?"

Morrison, Forbes reflected as he followed the general to the offices, was typical of many West Point men he had met. Their lives were the Army—in Morrison's case, the Air Force—and every waking moment was devoted to thoughts of military efficiency and national defense. At some early stage in life, it seemed, they made a decision to turn themselves into automatons; first to win an appointment to the Academy, then to graduate highest in their class. After that it was promotions, from lieutenant to captain, to major, and on up the ladder toward four-star general. To achieve the ultimate goal, a man must never smile. He must never joke, never engage in idle conversation, and he must demonstrate at all times, whether on duty or not, that he is thinking about the safety of the United States of America.

There was nothing wrong with such dedication. It certainly contributed to the security of the nation. But Harry sometimes wondered if it didn't leave some gaps in their lives. And maybe in their thinking. Two hours ago, when Forbes asked if they should hold the countdown before firing the satellite, Morrison hadn't hesitated an instant before saying no. The Air Force wanted the satellite launched, and it was to be launched at that specific time, and there were to be no deviations. Orders had been issued, and orders were to be obeyed. That was all there was to it.

And then, when the satellite exploded, the general had had the same shocked reaction as everyone else in the room. But there was also the cold look of suspicion on his face. The Russians? The Chinese? Sabotage? For a man who had spent his entire military career thinking about the country's possible enemies, and what they might be up to, the reaction was not so unusual, Harry supposed. Still, it had surprised him at the time.

Morrison held the office door open, then closed it firmly behind them after Harry entered. He stood with his back to the door for a moment, then fixed a hard gaze on Harry.

"That explosion up there was caused by some kind of spacecraft. Shortly after it was hit by the satellite, it entered the earth's atmosphere and landed in eastern Arizona. Norad tracked it. About an hour ago one of our helicopters found it."

Harry stared incredulously at the man. "What kind of a spacecraft?"

Morrison shifted his gaze to the floor and paced slowly across the room. "We don't know yet. From what they've told me, it doesn't appear to have been damaged from the landing. And to some degree, it is still functioning. At least its lights are still blinking on and off. But no signs of life have been observed. We've made no effort to enter it."

"My God, are you serious?! Some kind of flying saucer?"

Morrison nodded, continuing to pace. "Some kind of spacecraft. Nothing we have ever seen before."

Harry shook his head, too stunned to fully grasp the idea. Was it possible? After all the saucer sightings and all the wild stories about people from outer space, was it really true? It would be the most incredible thing since . . . There was nothing to compare it with. He lowered himself in a chair and blinked at Morrison. "Holy God, General, do you realize what this means?"

"Until we find out where it came from and why it was up there, we have no way of knowing what it means."

"Yes, but . . ." The general was right, of course. But by the way the thing maneuvered at such incredible speeds, it almost certainly came from outer space. And that meant that some kind of living thing had to have created it. Some form of life much more advanced than ours. "Have you told Washington?" Harry asked.

Morrison stopped pacing and leaned back against a desk, his manner still grim. "I've got a call in to the White House. To Gordon Cain, the president's chief of staff. This should go directly to the president."

Harry nodded. He realized suddenly that he was being told things that General Morrison normally would regard as top secret. Morrison was staring thoughtfully at him, as if waiting for the question. "What do you want with me?" Harry asked.

"I talked to the director," Morrison said. "He says you know Hangar 18 as well as anyone in NASA."

"Hangar 18?"

Morrison nodded. "I have the director's permission to move this thing, whatever it is, to that location. I've already ordered it done."

Hangar 18 was in the western part of Texas, a huge building that was once used by NASA to debrief space capsules. That was back in the days when they were uncertain about the capsules bringing back dangerous bacteria or unknown space poisons. The hangar was fully equipped with all the equipment and computers necessary for analyzing foreign materials. "It's the logical place," he said. "It's got all the facilities.

"I want you to be in charge of this," Morrison said. "I want you to go there and set up a team. Check this thing out thoroughly. Top to bottom, inside out."

Harry was surprised. Morrison had never displayed any particularly high regard for anyone in NASA before. But maybe he had no other choices. And the whole idea of their having picked up a flying saucer still seemed incredible to Harry. "Are you sure about this thing, General? That it's the same thing we saw on our radar?"

Morrison nodded. "After it left the shuttle, it entered our atmosphere and came down. Norad tracked it all the way."

Could it be a hoax? A new Russian spacecraft of some kind? It didn't seem likely. But it also seemed incredible that it could be something from outer space. On the other hand, what else could it be? "I'll be happy to do it, General." As quickly as he spoke, Harry felt a twinge of uneasiness. An alien spacecraft! Possibly with some kind of alien beings still inside of it!

"Good," Morrison said. "You realize, of course, that the capture of this thing is classified information. It is not to be discussed with anyone. Only those who absolutely need to know."

"Of course," Harry said. The general was right. Any premature announcement would bring thousands of press people. And probably millions of sightseers. There could even be a reaction of panic. "I'll need a considerable staff," he said.

"Whoever you want. Get the best you can find. Just so they understand that this is a top secret project."

Harry nodded, his mind whirling, sifting through the possibilities. He rose and moved for the door. "I'd better start making some phone calls, General."

After the door closed, General Morrison moved to the desk and sat down, considering the logistics of transporting the spacecraft to Texas. He had already ordered one of the big Sikorsky Skycrane choppers to Arizona to pick up the thing. But it would have to be refueled somewhere along the way. El Paso would be the logical place. The telephone buzzed and he quickly picked up the receiver.

"General Morrison," an operator said, "please hold on. I'm transferring your call to Mr. Cain at his home."

Morrison glanced at his watch. In Washington it was quarter to four in the morning.

The voice that answered the phone had no sleepiness in it. It might have been eight in the evening and Cain was sitting in front of the fire with a cocktail. "Hello, General," he said.

"I'm sorry to bother you at this hour, Mr. Cain, but . . ."

"It's quite all right. What can I do for you?"

"Sir, I'm at the NASA offices in Houston at the moment. I have some information I feel should go directly to the president as quickly as possible."

"I see. What is it?"

Morrison hesitated. He would have preferred talking to the president. But he knew Gordon Cain would not permit it without first hearing why. Morrison explained the situation as clearly as he could; from the appearance of the blips and the explosion over the space shuttle to the tracking of the spacecraft and its discovery in Arizona. When he finished, there was a long silence. Then Cain's voice was non-committal.

"I don't want to discuss this any further on the phone, General. You be at my office at ten in the morning."

"I think the president should hear about it as quickly as possible, Mr. Cain."

"I'll take care of that, General. You just be here at ten." The tone had turned cool, suggesting that Gordon Cain knew how to handle his job without any outside advice.

Morrison tried to keep the irritation out of his voice. "Very well, Mr. Cain. I'll be there."

"One hundred thousand feet," Capcom's voice announced quietly. "Descent angle, twenty-eight degrees. You're doing fine, Orbiter."

His hand now lightly gripping the stubby control stick, Lew Price glanced out the narrow windows.

31

From blue-black darkness, they were heading into a rosy sunrise. "Here it comes. Another day."

Bancroft smiled, but didn't look up. He was too engrossed in his instruments.

They were still seventy thousand feet above the clouds, but it looked like Florida was entirely in the clear. Plummeting downward at the rate of fifteen thousand feet per minute, the predictor dots on the screen in front of Price showed a long curving glide pattern toward the Cape.

"Sixty thousand feet," Capcom said. Then, a minute later, "Forty-five thousand."

The seventy-five-ton ship did not exactly handle like an F-16. But the controls responded well enough, and Price kept it perfectly on pattern.

They finally hit the high winds. But the turbulence was minimal, and the outline of Florida came clearly into view. Price banked the ship thirty degrees to the left, angling them more toward the coastal configuration he knew was Canaveral.

"Forty seconds," Capcom said. "Twenty seconds to final approach."

They were in the glide pattern, and it was now evident how fast the earth was rushing toward them.

"Final approach," Flight Activity said. "Twenty seconds. Two hundred and ninety knots. You're a little fast, Steve."

"Check," Steve answered.

Lew quickly punched buttons. "Speed brakes out. Gear down. Starting flare."

"Roger. Instruments and visuals confirm."

The runway was suddenly there—three miles of it rushing at them at two hundred miles an hour. Lew lifted the nose. A moment later there was a heavy thump, and Flight Activity said, "Touchdown."

The runway markers rushed past in colored blurs. Then Lew hit the brakes, throwing them heavily against their harnesses. The markers came into focus, flickering by slower and slower until finally they were stopped.

An ambulance and a NASA van pulled up to the side as they dropped out of the hatch. The NASA man, a tall string bean with a bald head, came jogging over, his face drawn with gloom. "Hey, I'm sorry about what happened up there," he said.

Lew nodded. "The line forms to the right."

"We'd like to see Gates' wife," Steve said. "And his kids."

The NASA man took their helmets and put them in the van. "Look, the Air Force'll take care of . . ."

Lew cut him off. "We don't care about the Air Force."

"Okay, okay. Take it up with Harry when you get to Houston. Your plane leaves in an hour."

While the NASA man watched, they helped take the body from the shuttle and put it in the ambulance. Then they all climbed into the van and drove to the terminal building in silence.

IV

The Bannon County Sheriff's Office was at the back of the courthouse, a musty little corner with three offices and a two-cell jail at the rear. The young deputy sitting at the front desk was doubtful about letting Sam Tate see the sheriff until he stated the purpose of his visit. Then Sheriff Dan Barlow's dry voice came through the open door. "Let him in, Ken. After all, Sam Tate is one of our best customers."

A buzzer sounded, letting Tate through a wooden gate. Once in the sheriff's office, he closed the door behind him. Dan Barlow was going through a stack of papers, a pair of horn-rimmed glasses resting far down on his nose. He was a burly man in his early fifties, his face creased and tanned from the desert. "Have a seat, Sam. What can we do for you?"

Tate had showered and shaved and put on a clean shirt and combed his hair. But Dan Barlow didn't seem to notice the difference. He gave Tate only a brief glance and continued studying the papers.

"Sheriff, you're not going to believe this. I mean, what I'm going to tell ya. What I saw last night."

"Probably not," Barlow answered. "Try me."

Tate didn't mention how much beer he had drunk. He said only that he was driving home about one o'clock when he saw the light cross the sky. Then he described in detail what happened after that. When he finished, Barlow was staring at him over the glasses.

"It's the honest to God's truth, Sheriff. That thing

was sitting there right behind the hill, and the lights were flashing on and off like a Christmas tree. I could see it plain as day in the moonlight. You gotta believe me, Sheriff."

Barlow took his glasses off. He eased back, propped his feet on the desk and folded his arms over his chest. "Sam," he said, "I hear what you're saying. But you got to admit you don't have the most dazzling reputation around here."

Tate knew what the sheriff was talking about. But he had never been so drunk that he saw elephants or spiders. Nor was that thing he saw last night an hallucination. "Sure," he admitted, "I had a couple beers over at Pete's. But I know what I saw. It was there, Sheriff. I coulda touched it."

Barlow smiled. "Why didn't ya?"

Touching it was the last thing that ever would have entered Tate's mind. "I was scared, I guess. You woulda been too."

Barlow gave him a narrow look. "Tell you this . . . if I were you I'd be scared from as much drinking and driving as you do. We've talked about this before, Sam."

Tate took a deep breath and let it out slowly, wishing he hadn't gone near Pete's last night, almost wishing he hadn't seen the damned flying saucer at all. Then his hopes lifted a little. "Remember about two months ago, Sheriff . . . the time when I run across those RV campers that was supposed to be stolen? Out there by Wells Canyon? You thought I was just being drunk. Or joking around. Remember?"

Barlow gazed thoughtfully at him for a minute. Then he rubbed the bridge of his nose and nodded. "I remember."

"I'll drive out with ya. You can see for yourself. Honest to God, Sheriff. That thing's up there."

The sheriff gave the papers on his desk a distasteful look. Then he sighed and pulled his feet off the desk. "Okay, Sam, let's go have a look."

They didn't say a word on the way. Passing Pete's Polish Palace, the sheriff gave Tate a sour glance. Then he fished a half-smoked cigar from his pocket and stuck it in his mouth. At the dirt road, he swung the police car off the highway and roared up the long slope at thirty miles an hour. When they reached the saddle, he rolled to a stop while the dust drifted past the car. Then he carefully lighted his cigar. Tate was out by then, circling to the driver's side.

"It's just down the slope there, Sheriff. You'll have to get out."

Barlow nodded and climbed out. He followed Tate farther up the road until they had a clear view of the entire hillside. There was nothing. The shallow area behind the rise contained nothing more than rocks and sand and a scattering of brush. While they stared at it, a jackrabbit scurried across the area and disappeared in a hole. Sam Tate was looking from right to left, then behind, then back to the stretch of flat ground, like a man who couldn't figure out where he was.

"Well?" Barlow said.

"It was here!" Sam said desperately. "It was here! Right here!"

The sheriff nodded. "Sure, sure."

"It was! It was!"

Tate headed down the slope, stumbling, then picking up speed. He ran over the rise and stopped where the flying saucer had been. He turned a complete circle, scratched his head, then stood with his hands on his hips, staring forlornly at the rocks and sand.

Dan Barlow gazed at the thunderhead of clouds gathering in the west. It looked like they might have some thunder showers this afternoon. He examined the end of his cigar, then headed slowly back to the car.

It was ten minutes to eleven, Washington, D.C., time, when General Morrison was finally ushered in for his ten o'clock appointment with Gordon Cain. The office was impressive: rich blue carpeting and a massive mahogany desk. Cain moved unhurriedly across the room, smiling, his hand extended. "Come in, General, come in. I'm awfully sorry I kept you waiting. Some urgent business for the president, I'm afraid."

"Of course," Morrison said.

Cain guided them to a corner where a coffee table was flanked by a white sofa and two winged chairs. "Sit down," he urged, and gestured to the couch. He drew up a chair for himself and lightly stroked his forehead, smiling easily. "Well, we seem to have ourselves a problem, don't we?" He gave Morrison a bland smile. "Hit us right out of the blue, so to speak."

There were a number of conflicting opinions about Gordon Cain and his position in the White House. *Time* magazine said he was the deadliest enemy any politician could have in Washington. Others said that without him the whole Tyler administration would collapse. There was no doubt he was a powerful man, and apparently he had the complete confidence of the president.

There was nothing menacing in his appearance. He was about forty-five, a neatly dressed man who looked very much like the hundreds of other ambitious young-executive types who seemed to flock to Washington. In matters dealing with the Air Force, Morrison had always found him helpful and efficient.

"Yes," Morrison agreed. "And I think it could be a very serious problem. Have you told the president?"

Cain gazed thoughtfully at the coffee table for a moment, then shook his head. "Not yet," he said.

Morrison stared at him. "Mr. Cain . . . a thing like this."

"I know, I know," Cain said quietly. "The president had to fly to Boston early this morning for a swing through New England. He has a rally at the Garden in New York tonight."

"Nevertheless . . ."

"Tomorrow," Cain went on, "it's Ohio, Michigan,

Illinois . . . At the moment, General, he has enough on his mind with the election without my dropping something like this on him." Cain smiled as if that settled the matter, then shifted in the chair. "Where is the spacecraft now?"

"Hangar 18," Morrison answered. "It was delivered about an hour ago."

"Hangar 18? Where's that?"

"In Texas. Wolf Air Force Base. NASA took it over some years ago and converted the hangar into a manned lunar receiving station."

"And it'll work?"

Morrison wasn't sure what the question meant. "It's got all the facilities," he said. "Chemical, engineering, biological labs. Decontamination chambers, computer centers, . . . completely equipped hospital—everything we'll need."

"Sounds good."

Morrison wondered if he had flown all the way to Washington to answer these simple questions. He had expected to be ushered in to see the president. At the very least, he expected to hear President Tyler's reaction to the situation, and to receive some specific orders about procedure. He wondered if Gordon Cain understood the magnitude of their discovery. "The president should issue a statement," he said.

"A statement?"

"To the public," Morrison added. "Without telling where we're keeping the spacecraft, of course." Cain rose and moved slowly toward his desk, apparently contemplating the question. "That's where it gets a little sticky, General."

"I know. We can't risk a panic. But if he worded a statement in the right way, it could . . ."

"It's really not that simple," Cain interrupted. He turned and moved back to the coffee table, frowning thoughtfully at the carpet. He drew his chair a few inches closer to Morrison and sat down again, this time leaning forward, his manner intimate and confidential.

"You've seen the latest opinion polls, haven't you, General? Gallup, Harris, the rest of them? They're saying this election is too close to call. Anything could tip it one way or the other in these last couple of weeks."

The last thing Morrison wanted to discuss was the subject of opinion polls and the upcoming presidential election. Aside from the candidates' proposals concerning the defense budget, he rarely took any active interest in politics. A good many army officers had blown promising careers by making that mistake. Nor could he understand how politics was in any way relevant to the problems surrounding the discovery of what was probably an alien spacecraft.

"I'm afraid I don't understand what you're driving at, Mr. Cain."

Gordon Cain smiled, apparently amused by Morrison's political naiveté.

"It seems that you have forgotten, General. Or perhaps you are not aware of the statements the president's opponent made shortly after his party nominated him for president."

Morrison shook his head, baffled.

"In September, Senator Stoddard publicly stated that he once saw a UFO."

Morrison stared at the man, still not seeing the full significance.

"After he made the statement," Cain went on, "the president went after him on it. He asked the public if they would feel safe electing a man who believed in flying saucers. The next week, Stoddard dropped seven points in the polls. It was a big joke." Cain smiled and gave a half shrug. "So what do you think it would do to the president's chances for re-election if the public found out there's an alien spacecraft parked in this NASA facility? It would suddenly make Senator Stoddard appear to be an oracle. And President Tyler, having ridiculed the senator, would look very foolish."

Morrison rose and moved slowly away from the sofa, considering the matter. *Damn,* he thought. The presidential election was still irrelevant to the question of the spacecraft. But he could appreciate the awkwardness of Gordon Cain's—and the president's—position. "Yes," he said, "I see your problem."

Cain rose and moved toward his desk. "So what can we do about it?"

Morrison had no idea what to do about it. "It's too late to call off the investigation of the ship," he pointed out. "We wouldn't want to anyway. We have to know what the thing is."

"Of course we do," Cain agreed. "I'm not asking you to do that. All I'm asking is if we can keep this under wraps for two weeks. Just until the election is over."

Two weeks was not a long time, Morrison reflected. And keeping the discovery quiet for a short period was certainly justifiable.

Cain was gazing solemnly at him. "And I might remind you of something, General. I think you know what it would mean for this country if Senator Stoddard were elected president. What he'd do to the defense budget."

Senator Stoddard's position on the defense budget was the only thing Morrison knew about the man. He had been attacking the Department of Defense for the past three years, claiming the high defense budget was the cause of inflation, unemployment, crop failures, and every other problem facing the country. If elected, he was promising a thirty percent reduction in the defense budget—along with a stronger military force. Apparently enough people had bought such pie-in-the-sky nonsense that it looked like he had a good chance of beating the incumbent president. Morrison nodded. "It would be a disaster."

"Exactly," Cain answered.

"I can order the Air Force to take over security at Hanger 18," Morrison suggested. "There are living quarters there. The NASA team doesn't have to come and go. That would prevent any information leaks."

Cain was nodding. "I'd appreciate it, General. And I know the president will too."

"There's one problem," Morrison said.

"What?"

"Bancroft and Price. The crew on the shuttle. They say they saw something up there, and that the satellite hit it."

Cain frowned. "Will they talk?"

"If you saw a satellite hit a UFO, wouldn't you talk about it?"

"Yes," Cain admitted. "But can't you keep them quiet for a couple of weeks?"

"I don't know," Morrison said, remembering his brief meeting with the two men. He had always been a little uncomfortable around NASA people. The informal manner in which they ran their operation tended to make him uneasy. And the astronauts like Price and Bancroft seemed to be the least disciplined among them. "They're mavericks," he said. "They're NASA and proud of it. If I ordered them not to talk, I'm inclined to think they'd tell me to stuff it."

Cain nodded thoughtfully. "All right. Let me worry about them." He glanced at his watch, smiled and extended his hand. "I'm due in a meeting. Thanks for your help, General. I really do appreciate it."

"I'll keep in touch," Morrison said as he was ushered out the door.

"Please do, General." After the door closed, Gordon Cain moved back to his desk and picked up the phone. He thought for a minute, then dialed.

A cold, somewhat bored voice answered. "Lafferty."

"Gordon Cain. I want to see you."

"Where?"

"The park. Eight o'clock."

"Okay," the voice said, and the phone clicked off.

"I'm sorry it turned out that way," Harry Forbes said. "It's just one of those things, and there was nothing you could do about it. So don't start feeling guilty about it. You're both good shuttle men—the best—and we need you. So why don't you just take a few days off and forget about it."

There was something strange about Harry's behavior, Steve Bancroft decided. There was something on his mind, something he wasn't telling them about.

They had found him in his office, going through a thick manila folder of papers, making notes on a legal pad. When Lew and Steve came in, he had placed the folder and the pad in a drawer and closed it. There was nothing hurried about the movement. But it was still obvious he didn't want them to see the notes. For people who were as close as the three of them had always been, it was a strange thing for Harry to do.

They had talked about Colonel Judd Gates and his family for a few minutes. Then Lew had brought up the unidentified spacecraft that had hovered over them. It was at that point Harry seemed to avoid looking directly at them anymore. He looked at the desk top, or swiveled his chair off to one side, looking anywhere but at them.

"It's hard to say what happened," he said. "We don't know for sure. Maybe we never will know. It's possible, of course, that the satellite's rockets were defective."

"It hit something, Harry," Bancroft said, "some kind of spacecraft. You saw the radar blips."

Harry nodded. "Yes, we all saw the blips. But that doesn't necessarily mean it was a spacecraft. The blips could have been caused by some kind of space phenomena we don't understand. The same thing could have caused the explosion."

Lew stared at him in disbelief. "It was a spacecraft, Harry. I saw it, Steve saw it, Gates saw it!"

Harry nodded. "I know, Lew, I know."

"Why don't we run the telemetry tapes?" Steve suggested.

Harry shook his head as if he were tired of the

whole thing. "It's not necessary. We already know what's on them. We've run them a dozen times already. It'll all be put in the report."

"Harry, it was a spacecraft, damn it," Lew said emphatically. "It was hovering less than two hundred feet above us, and all three of us saw it. And we're not a bunch of looneys trying to get some kind of publicity, or having hallucinations."

Harry sighed and held up his hand. "Look, I don't doubt what you saw, and I believe you. There were blips on the radar screens, and you saw the thing. So a report is being written, and everything will be in it. Believe me. And that's all you need to know for now. Everything's going to be all right."

"Harry . . ."

"It's going to be all right," Harry repeated before Bancroft could go on. "Trust me. Okay?"

Steve looked at Lew and got a resigned shrug in return. Harry had always been honest with them. If the report didn't come out right, there was no doubt he would see that it was corrected. And they were fully aware of the bureaucratic red tape that sometimes tied Harry into knots. Steve shrugged. "Okay."

Harry seemed relieved. "That's better," he said with a smile. "Now, why don't you take it easy and go up to Dallas or over to New Orleans for a couple days?"

Gordon Cain hated the fact that people like Lafferty were necessary. Even more, he hated the fact that he had to deal with them. But without them, it was almost impossible to survive in Washington anymore. Now that forty congressmen were watching everything they did, the CIA was totally off limits for any White House work. The FBI was even worse. With the Freedom of Information Act, a Russian spy could demand copies of FBI files, and by law the Bureau was required to turn them over.

The first contact with Lafferty had come two

years ago, on a matter involving a relatively minor problem. During the off-year elections a campaign party worker's briefcase had been stolen during a flight from Miami to Washington, D.C. Under normal circumstances, it was a case of simple theft. In this instance, however, the briefcase contained a complete list of big donors to the party, along with a schedule showing how the money was to be filtered out to various congressional candidates. There was nothing illegal about what was being done. But if the information had been made public, it would have proven extremely embarrassing for both the donors and the candidates. And as the theft occurred six days before the election, there would have been no time to explain anything.

John Bernard, the president's legal counsel, had proposed the solution for the problem. Rather than reporting the incident to the police or the FBI, and risk the documents being exposed, he suggested they contact a man named Lafferty. Lafferty was a former CIA man who, with a number of other former agents and FBI men, had started a sort of quasi private detective agency called Allied Research Services. From what John Bernard had heard, the company was very good at handling the kind of problem they had. They were also very discreet. And as they could provide volumes of research material on any subject, there was no difficulty in justifying the payments for their services.

When Cain made the first call to them, Lafferty refused to come to the White House to discuss the problem. Instead, he had Cain meet him in the terminal of Dulles Airport, and they discussed the problem while sitting in the American Airlines departure lounge.

It was a chilling experience for Cain. Except for his eyes, there was nothing extraordinary about Lafferty's appearance. He was neatly dressed in a dark suit, a moderately large man wearing heavy, black-rimmed glasses that made him look more like a bookkeeper than an undercover agent. But behind the glasses, the eyes were like two chunks of glacial ice.

Through their twenty-minute conference, he spoke no more than two dozen words, grunting occasionally, sometimes nodding his head a quarter of an inch. He spent most of the time staring at the other people, as if he were making mental notes for future use.

"No problem," he said when Cain finished outlining the situation. "It'll be ten thousand dollars. How do you propose to pay?"

Cain then explained how they could use a quick voter-preference poll in Maryland, and that ten thousand dollars would not be an unreasonable fee for such a service.

"You'll have it tomorrow," Lafferty said, then added, "In the future, you might think about our doing research work directly for the government. No point in using the party's money." With that, he gave Cain an icy glance, then rose and walked away.

The briefcase arrived at the White House two days later, the contents apparently undisturbed. Three months later there was some other delicate problem requiring Lafferty's services. Then five or six more occasions after that. What surprised Cain was the discovery that Allied Research Services was well known around Washington, and was used by dozens of congressmen and other government departments. According to John Bernard, they employed more than a hundred agents, and their annual gross income from governmental research projects alone was over ten million dollars.

Lafferty hadn't changed in the six or eight months since Cain had last seen him. Cain's chauffeur turned right off of Massachusetts Avenue and entered Rock Creek Park at exactly eight o'clock. Three minutes later they saw Lafferty at the side of his black sedan, standing patiently, his hands at his sides as if ready for action. The chauffeur pulled in behind and switched off the lights. Cain still found the sight of Lafferty chilling.

"It's been a long time," the man said quietly as he slid into the back seat.

"Yes," Cain answered.

"What can I do for you?"

Cain switched on the interior light and handed over a manila envelope. Lafferty slid out the two glossy photographs. He gazed expressionlessly at them for a minute, then looked at Cain.

"Their names are Lew Price and Steve Bancroft," Cain said. "The round-faced one is Price."

"The crew of that shuttle that got in trouble?"

"Yes," Cain answered.

"What's the problem?"

Cain took a deep breath, wishing he didn't have to do this. "They're civilians. There's no way to officially keep them quiet. They may talk about the accident—what happened up there. If they do, I don't want anybody to believe what they say."

"What are they likely to say?"

"That they saw something . . . an unidentified flying object."

It was the closest Cain had ever seen Lafferty come to smiling. But it still didn't amount to much, no more than a faint twitch at one corner of the mouth. "That all?" Lafferty asked.

"That's all."

Lafferty slid the photos back in the envelope and pushed the door open. "Consider it done," he said and slammed the door behind him.

It was a matter of control, Cain reflected as he watched Lafferty return to his car. In the White House there were a hundred staff people whose loyalty to Cain and to the president was beyond question. No matter what kind of crisis might arise, Cain knew none of them would question an order, or fail to carry it out. It was this loyalty and control that was missing with Lafferty. Men like him had no loyalties; neither to people nor to principles. If the opposition paid them more money, they would be equally ruthless in dealing with Gordon Cain—or the president—or anyone else who appeared to be an obstruction to their client. Lafferty was part of a new breed in America, Cain decided. Or maybe he was the latest model of a breed that had been evolving for a long time. They were the new executives of efficiency. Nothing mattered except getting the job done.

V

Steve Bancroft didn't know how to respond to the signal that was coming up from Mission Control. It was a harsh ringing that echoed deafeningly through the cockpit. It must be some kind of an alarm. He turned to the left and right, then opened his eyes wide.

He was staring at the ceiling of his bedroom. He blinked, still not awake, and reached for the telephone as it rang for the third time. "Hullo," he said with a thick voice.

"Steve?" a female voice said. "This is Flo."

Steve drew himself higher in the bed and rested on an elbow. "Who?" he asked, still not quite down to earth yet. The sun was slanting brightly through the window, telling him he had slept late. Normal people suffered from jet lag. When he came down from a shuttle flight, it took him twenty-four hours to figure out what day it was.

"Flo Matson," the voice said. "In Public Information."

Steve cleared his throat. "Oh. Yeah. Good morning, Flo."

"The same to you. But I don't think it's going to be very long. Have you seen the morning paper?"

"No."

"Well, take a look at it. Then you and Lew better get over here."

"Why? What's it say?"

"I'll see you in about an hour," she said and hung up.

Steve put the phone back in its cradle and frowned at the window. He had no idea what she could be talking about. He swung his legs out of bed and scratched his head for a minute, reminding himself his name was Steven L. Bancroft. Then he headed for the bathroom.

He showered and shaved, feeling no urgency about Flo's call. The story of Colonel Gates' being killed had already been in the evening papers and on all the TV news shows. Nothing could be worse than that.

He was two blocks down the street in the booth of a coffee shop when he saw the story. He had bought a newspaper outside the restaurant and ordered his breakfast before he looked at the front page. The feature story was about Colonel Gates and how he had died on the flight. The other story, and the one Flo Matson was no doubt talking about, was on the lower half of the page. Steve stared at the headline, feeling his first sip of coffee turn to acid in his stomach. SHUTTLE DEATH BLAMED ON NASA CREW, it said.

He couldn't believe it. And the text of the story was even more ridiculous: "The death of Colonel Judd Gates during a shuttle flight Tuesday and Wednesday, was unquestionably due to the negligence of the two NASA crew members, pilot Lewis Price and shuttle commander Steve Bancroft, according to an unnamed Air Force spokesman. While the two crew members were in the process of launching a satellite from the shuttle, Colonel Gates was allowed to remain in the exposed cargo bay, thus causing his immediate death from flying debris when the satellite mysteriously exploded. The procedure was contrary to all safety regulations, the highly placed source insisted late last night. 'The colonel's death,' he stated, 'was clearly due to negligence on the part of the two NASA astronauts.'

To date, NASA officials have been unavailable for comment.

"Colonel Gates, 42, a nineteen-year veteran of . . ."

Steve slammed the newspaper on the table and strode angrily to the telephone at the back of the restaurant. Lew answered the phone with the first ring.

"Lew . . . ?"

"Yeah! Did you read this goddamned story on the front page of the paper?!" He was almost screaming.

"Yeah, I read it. Now take it easy, Lew. Flo Matson wants to talk to us. Can you be there in a half hour?"

"I'll be there in five minutes!"

Flo Matson was not screaming. But she was clearly as disturbed about the story as Price and Bancroft. She was a former newspaperwoman, a tough, slightly overweight, dishwater blonde in her late thirties. "The damnable part of it is," she said, pacing behind her desk, "I can't even find out where the story came from. There's no byline on it. And the newspaper won't tell me a thing. Nor does anyone at the Air Force claim to know anything about it."

Lew had calmed down a little. He was slouched in a chair, his intertwined fingers across his nose, squinting narrowly at the window. "At best, the story is slanderous," he said. "We had no control over when that satellite was fired. If anyone was responsible, it was Morrison. He insisted the damned thing be launched."

"Don't bother trying to prove that," Flo said. "And I think we'd better save things like that for an official inquiry." She shrugged. "If there is one." She stopped behind her desk and shook her head. "I don't get it. Who'd float a story like that?"

"The Air Force, honey," Lew muttered.

"Why?"

Steve gave a soft snort. "The first five hundred articles of Air Force regulations read 'In case of trouble, cover your ass.' But this is stupid."

"They'll never get away with it."

Flo's anger suddenly flared again. "But they're saying you guys are responsible for wrecking a satellite! . . . And killing a man!"

"We didn't do anything," Steve said flatly. "The satellite hit something. And we can prove it."

"How?" Flo asked.

"It's on the tapes," Lew said. "They saw the blips over at Mission Control, the same as we did. And that thing came right over the shuttle and stopped."

"Then you'd better get those tapes," Flo said. "In fact, why don't you bring a copy over here. Maybe I can get permission to release them to the TV networks."

Things were quiet at Mission Control. There was only one technician working at a computer, a man Steve and Lew didn't know. But the tapes were still in the monitoring console.

"Thirty-one hours and ten minutes," Steve said when Lew inserted the final tape of the series. Lew pressed the "fast forward" button, and the digital timer blurred through the numbers. He finally found the time they wanted and punched the replay button.

"Okay, here we go."

The blip of the orbiting shuttle came onto the screen, moving slowly across from right to left.

"Six seconds," Steve said, keeping one eye on the timer. "Five . . . four . . ."

"Where is it?" Lew asked. Nothing more than the shuttle's lonely blip continued across the screen.

"Three . . . two . . . one . . ."

"Where's the blip?! There's nothing!"

Steve frowned, a feeling of heaviness starting to slide into his stomach. "Play it again."

Lew ran the tape back to 31:10:00 and started again. They both watched in silence this time, their suspicions growing. Again there was nothing but the shuttle. Lew banged the "stop" button and stared at Steve.

"Either we imagined the whole thing," Steve said, ". . . or the blip of the UFO's been erased."

"We didn't imagine it," Lew said emphatically. "Let's go talk to Harry."

Going up the elevator to Harry's office, the heavy feeling in Steve's stomach grew even worse. He should have known it yesterday, he realized. From the moment they had walked into Harry's office, he knew something was funny—Harry carefully sticking the pad and the manila folder in the drawer, . . . the evasiveness, . . . Harry insisting they not run the tape again. My God, he couldn't believe it. Could Harry have had something to do with that story appearing in the paper? No. Harry might have had something on his mind. But he wouldn't do a thing like that.

There was no secretary at the desk. They strode past and pushed the door open, Steve in the lead. "Harry . . . ?"

The man at the desk was not Harry. He was five years older, a portly man with steel-rimmed glasses and a hairline receding to the middle of his skull. He was as startled as they were.

"Where's Harry?" Lew asked.

The man turned away and started shoving things into the desk drawers. "Gone," he said.

"Gone?"

"Gone where?" Lew asked.

"He's been reassigned," the man said.

"What're you talking about?"

"I just told you," the man said irritably.

"Where'd he go?"

"I don't know. It's classified. Top secret."

"When will he be back?"

"I have no idea. Look, do you mind? This is my office now, and I'm busy."

Steve glanced quickly around, realizing that Harry was indeed gone. His prize possession, a photograph of himself riding on the shoulders of Neil Armstrong and Buzz Aldrin, was no longer on the wall. "Yeah," he said to the man, "sorry." He followed Lew out and closed the door behind them.

"We've been framed, buddy," Lew said.

Steve picked up the secretary's phone and dialed three digits. "Is this Mr. Cameron's office?" he said when a girl answered.

"No, sir," she said sweetly, "Mr. Cameron is on a new assignment. Mr. Halleck is temporarily replacing him. Would you like to speak to Mr. Halleck?"

"No. Can you tell me where I can get in touch with Mr. Cameron?"

"I'm sorry, I don't have that information. Perhaps if you called Mr. Forbes' office . . ."

"Yeah, I'll do that. Thanks." Steve returned the phone to the cradle and nodded. "Yep . . . I think you may be right."

"Let's get out of here," Lew said, and headed for the elevator.

Steve followed him, trying to make some sense out of the whole thing. He still couldn't believe that Harry Forbes would be a part of a cover-up to protect the Air Force. Harry was the proudest member of their NASA team. He never showed it, but he was like a football coach working twelve hours a day to teach his players every technique in the game. When they won, he smiled quietly and showed little emotion. But it was always apparent that down deep he was the happiest man on earth. And when things didn't go right, he always blamed himself rather than his crew. No, Harry wouldn't have had anything to do with an Air Force cover-up. So what the hell was going on?

"You know, buddy," Lew said when they reached their cars in the parking lot, "if they hang this on us, we're through. And not just with NASA."

Steve rested an elbow on the roof of Lew's car and looked thoughtfully at the big eight-story NASA building.

"In fact, we're through, period," Lew added. "We couldn't get a part-time job flying a kite."

Steve nodded. "And Harry said we didn't have anything to worry about. What do you suppose he meant by that? 'Trust me,' he said."

"Do you think he knew anything about the doctored telemetry?"

"All I know for sure is that we're being made the fall guys, and I don't like it."

"Maybe it's time we go to the newspapers with a story."

"What story?" Steve said. "We don't have a story, Lew. We claim the satellite hit a UFO. All the Air Force does is pull out the fake telemetry, and we look like idiots. Case closed."

Lew gave him a sour smile. "You're very encouraging."

"The whole thing's got to have something to do with that UFO. And that UFO is the only thing we've got going for us. That damned thing must have landed somewhere. At least when we last saw it, it looked like it was in trouble."

"And maybe turned into flaming dust entering the earth's atmosphere."

Steve shook his head. "I doubt it. A thing that could travel that fast, and reverse its direction like a Ping-Pong ball wouldn't have any trouble with atmospheric burnout."

"So what do we do? Put an ad in the paper? 'Would the people who were driving the UFO over the South Atlantic Wednesday afternoon please contact us?'"

Steve wasn't listening. He was still leaning on the car, still staring distantly at the NASA building. "Lew," he said, "wasn't Crown Mountain monitoring us, too?"

Lew shrugged. "Should have been. They always do."

"Figure there's any chance their telemetry hasn't been monkeyed with yet?"

Lew suddenly brightened. "Hey, it's worth a shot. I know a guy at Crown Mountain. George Turner. He was at Northwestern with me."

Steve smiled. "Why don't you introduce me?"

Lew gave him a doubtful frown. "Well, I'm not sure he's your type. He's much shorter than you. And a lousy dancer."

Phil Cameron felt his pulse quicken as they turned off the highway and headed up the narrow road toward Wolf Air Force Base. Within a matter of minutes they would be at NASA's Hangar 18.

The question of what he would see once they arrived there had kept his brain whirling until well after three o'clock in the morning. What would the thing look like? A saucer? A space capsule? Something like a shuttle? And where had it come from? How many millions or billions of miles had it traveled to reach earth? Had it just arrived here, making its first tentative probes around the planet when the satellite crashed into it? Or, along with dozens of sister ships, had it already made many visits to the earth? And what kind of beings might be piloting it? Friendly? Unfriendly? Little green men? Spider-like creatures? Might they be giants by our standards? Or maybe creatures so small we could carry them in the palms of our hands. Or maybe they weren't creatures at all. Maybe some kind of protoplasmic mass, or ooze that was completely foreign to our conception of advanced life?

He had even considered the possibility that the craft had not come from a distant galaxy at all, but might be a product of some country on earth. It was conceivable, of course, that the Russians could have made some scientific breakthrough: some giant leap forward that enabled them to manipulate time and space and the speed of travel. But such discoveries generally did not come without warning. A theory would be proposed here, a counter-theory there, and then the give and take of ideas, with some chemist or physicist stumbling across an unexplainable phenomenon in an obscure laboratory. That would be the opening. Then, like dandelion seeds drifting into a thousand fertile minds, the big leap would come. But there had been no evidence of such a breakthrough in the world. No, Cameron had decided, it was not likely that the craft was earth-based.

The previous afternoon, when Harry Forbes called him into his office and told him the Air Force had found the UFO and already transported it to Hangar 18, Cameron had been speechless. Harry had grinned and paced the office, so excited he could hardly talk straight.

"Imagine it, Phil, a flying saucer . . . a UFO . . . something from outer space! A contact from the outer world . . . from some other galaxy . . . maybe from some galaxy we don't even know exists! And we've got it! The thing we've all dreamed about . . . the thing we've never really believed would ever happen!"

"Holy God," was all Cameron could manage to say.

"They're leaving it up to us, Phil," Harry went on. "Morrison's putting me in charge of investigating the thing, examining it. So we've got to do it right. The best experts from every field. And I want you to come along. I need your help. So get your bags packed."

"When?"

"I'm leaving in about an hour. Can you come up first thing in the morning?"

"Yes. Sure."

"And figure on at least a week. Wrap up anything you've got going around here tonight. I've arranged for Nick Halleck to take over your job, and Joe Merrick is flying in from the Cape tonight to sit in for me. So, listen, you'd better get going. I've got a lot of phone calls to make."

"Harry?"

"Yeah?"

"Where in the hell is Hangar 18?"

Harry had laughed, finally realizing he was moving in four directions at the same time. "It's at what used to be Wolf Air Force Base, in west Texas, about fifty miles east of Midland. We used to use it for a lunar receiving lab. Look, there's an 8:15 A.M. flight to Midland. Just catch that, and I'll have an Air Force car pick you up."

"Is the Air Force going to be involved in this?"

"No. Just for guard duty and running errands. Don't worry about it, Phil. It's going to be our show all the way."

Midland, Texas, was in a dry, flat expanse of colorless dirt, the monotony broken only by the peppering of oil derricks as far as the eye could see. As quickly as Cameron stepped off the plane, two gray-blue uniformed Air Force MP's strode forward with questioning looks.

"Excuse me, sir, are you Mr. Cameron?"

"Yes," Cameron said. Neither of them could have been more than nineteen years old.

"I'm Corporal Thomas, and this is Private Maddox, sir. If you'll follow me, Private Maddox will get your bags."

With Cameron in the back seat, and the two young Air Force MP's sitting stiffly in front, they had driven silently eastward for forty-five minutes before the corporal finally slowed down and swung off the highway. Five minutes later Cameron could see the mass of army barracks rising on a broad knoll.

It was apparent that the place had been abandoned some time ago. The paint on the barracks was weathered and peeling, and the whole area was a foot deep in brown weeds. The corporal rolled to a slow stop at the gate, and an armed guard stepped from the sentry box to give them a close look. He nodded, said something into a walkie-talkie, and the corporal drove on.

Once they were past the empty barracks, the broad, open stretch of concrete runways was suddenly visible. There was a dusty, forlorn look to it, a forgotten tribute to some bygone time. Gusts of wind sent tumbleweeds skittering across the sun-bleached concrete and into the patches of dried weeds.

And then he saw it: the huge corrugated iron building standing in the midst of a dozen smaller hangars and utility sheds. "Is that it?" Cameron asked, "Hangar 18?" He had expected something a little fancier—more like the modern NASA building in Houston.

"Yes, sir," the corporal answered, and turned down a narrow strip of asphalt.

The thing looked more like a barn than a hangar, a giant, over-sized iron barn covering at least an acre of ground. Cameron's heart began to pound again as he thought about what was inside of it. Two minutes later they turned a corner, rolled across a broad concrete apron and came to a stop twenty yards from the huge, steel doors.

The doors were closed. Two army jeeps were parked on the apron, and guards with automatic weapons slung on their shoulders were patrolling the area. They gave Cameron suspicious glances as he stepped out of the car. Then Harry Forbes came grinning out of a tiny door off to the side.

"This was the lunar receiving lab?" Cameron asked when Harry reached the car.

Harry laughed, apparently still as excited as he had been the previous afternoon. "Don't let the outside fool you. That's just security. But it's a first-class operation inside. Come on. They'll bring your bags."

Harry took him through the small door and past a room piled high with crates and boxes. Then they were in a room where three technicians were sitting at consoles. In front of them, a broad window looked out at the interior of the hangar.

The hangar looked even larger on the inside, a cavernous, open area rising into a network of steel girders high above. On either side, the two levels of offices all had banks of windows overlooking the testing area in the center. But the hangar was so dark Cameron could see only a massive shadow in the center of the floor. At the bottom of it, a row of amber lights was blinking on and off, giving the whole area an eerie look.

"Okay," Harry said to one of the technicians, "let's have a look."

The man reached to the side and pushed a gang switch, suddenly illuminating the interior of the hangar with floodlights. Cameron caught his breath and stared, his heart once again pounding.

It was not saucer-shaped. Nor was it as sleek and modern-looking as he had expected. On a beveled base that rose about three feet from the floor, the "above deck" portion looked like four massive, domed-top modules clustered around a larger central module. It was all black, a glistening onyx-like black that gave it a heavy, utilitarian appearance. Each of the modules seemed to have a different kind of apparatus on the exterior. Some looked like banks of cooling pipes, some like louvres, others like patterns of miniature radar scanners. None of it was like anything Cameron had ever seen before. He shook his head, finally taking a breath. "I've heard all the crazy stories about UFOs, like everybody else. And I didn't believe them."

Harry nodded, understanding. "It's not the kind of thing most people want to believe in."

"Is there any exterior damage?"

"No," Harry said in a measured tone, "we think it was a controlled landing."

Cameron looked sharply at him. "That means someone brought it in. Someone must have landed it."

Harry nodded solemnly, knowing very well what

Cameron was thinking. It was exactly what he had concluded. "And that means someone is still aboard."

Cameron stared at the thing again, his imagination placing people—creatures?—in each of the modules. Were they staring out of a hole somewhere? Or watching with a remote camera, wondering the same things their captors were wondering? Cameron's throat suddenly felt dry. "How can we . . . ?"

"We'll find out when the others get here."

"Who's coming?" Cameron asked. He still couldn't take his eyes off the thing.

"Besides a team of NASA technicians and engineers," Harry said, "there's Neal Kelso, a linguist."

"For translations?"

"Right. And two doctors, Sarah Michaels and Paul Bannister . . . just in case."

Cameron nodded. "I wonder what they're like." He smiled weakly and added, "On second thought, I'm not sure I want to know."

Harry nodded. "I know what you mean."

VI

In Grace's Diner, Sam Tate had taken a stool at the far end of the counter to eat his lunch. He wasn't interested in talking to any more people. He had talked to enough of them in the last two days. In fact, he had talked to too many. He should have kept his mouth shut and not even mentioned the flying saucer. He had even called Herb Pope in Washington, D.C.

Huh, he thought, as he pushed a spoonful of beef stew into his mouth. Calling Herb Pope had been a big waste of money. A man comes around talking like he's just one of the boys and all he wants to do is run for Congress so he can bring some common sense to all those bureaucrats in Washington. Then he no sooner gets elected, and he's all of a sudden just as high and mighty and standoffish as the rest of them. Hell, the idiot probably didn't even know where Arizona was anymore.

"What did you say your name is again?" he kept asking after Sam had told him the story. Then, "Well, what I would suggest, Mr. Tate, is that you tell the local sheriff about it. Dan Barlow's his name. You just tell Dan that Herb Pope sent you. I'm sure he'll look into it."

"Dan Barlow already looked into it, Mr. Pope. But, you see, the saucer had taken off again when we got out there. But it was there, by God. A big black thing with yellow lights flashing on and off."

"I see. Well, you've done your duty, Mr. Tate.

61

You did what any good citizen would have done. You can be proud of yourself. And rest assured, I'll make a full report of it to the Defense Department."

"But, Mr. Pope . . ."

And that was the end of the conversation. Herb Pope would make a full report of it to the Defense Department. Hell, he hadn't even asked where Sam had seen the thing.

"How's the stew, Sam?" Rudy Millar had come out of the kitchen with a soup spoon and rested an elbow on the counter in front of him.

"S'good," Sam said.

Rudy was grinning at him, suddenly leaning close. "You see any more saucers, Sam? Any little purple people?"

Sam finished up the last bite of stew and dropped the spoon on the counter. "You can laugh all you wanna, but I know what I seen!"

"I believe you, Sam. Hell, I've seen saucers flyin' all over my kitchen. The other day, Grace threw one from clear over there by the cigarette machine."

Tate pulled two dollars from his wallet and threw them on the counter as he rose. "Ah . . . What do you know!" he said and strode for the door.

He went directly to his car, sucking on his teeth, realizing now that he hadn't gotten a toothpick on his way out. To hell with 'em, he thought. Maybe one of these days a whole squadron of saucers would come down and squash the lot of them.

"Mr. Tate?"

He hadn't noticed the two men angling across the parking lot toward him. They were both wearing black suits and striped neckties; both about thirty-five. They looked like easterners. "Yeah?" Sam said cautiously. "What about it?"

They were both smiling suddenly. The taller man rested a hand on the roof of Sam's car. "We've been looking all over for you, Mr. Tate. Mr. Keller was telling us how good you are with horses."

Sam glanced suspiciously from one to the other. Mr. Keller had never said anything especially complimentary to him about the way he handled the horses. "That so?" he said.

"Yes, he did," the tall man said. "And the fact is, our boss is looking for a good horse handler. He's just moved out to California, and he asked us to send him a good, reliable man. He'll double whatever Mr. Keller is paying you, Sam. Plus free room and board. What do you say?"

"Well, . . ." Sam looked across the street where a shiny new car was parked. It looked expensive. He wondered if Mr. Keller really had told them he was a good horse handler. Maybe he had. And the fact was, he had been sort of thinking about going out to California anyway. Considering the way he had been treated around here the last couple days, any place else would be better. "Well," he said, "I reckon I'd better tell Mr. Keller first. Get my things."

"That won't be necessary," the shorter man said. "We've already told him. And the boss told us to give you two hundred dollars to buy some new clothes. If we hurry, we can catch the next flight out of Tucson."

Sam scratched his head, feeling like things were moving awfully fast. "How about m'car?" he asked.

"Don't worry about it. We'll sell it and send you the money."

"Okay. Sure. Yeah, let's get going."

The technicians arrived first; nine more were from Houston, and four from the Cape. Phil Cameron watched their faces as they got their first look at the spacecraft. The reactions were the same as his had been: awe, mixed with fear and excitement. They were highly trained and experienced experts who knew what was real and what was fantasy—at least within the boundaries of technological advancements on earth. Staring at the spacecraft, they knew those boundaries would soon be extended far beyond anything they could have imagined.

The two medical doctors arrived next—Sarah Michaels, a slender, attractive woman in her mid-thirties, and Paul Bannister, a stocky man with a thick, black, well-trimmed beard. Sarah Michaels shook her head, too stunned to speak as she gazed at the spacecraft.

"You say there's probably somebody . . . something, still alive in there?" Bannister asked.

"Good Lord," Sarah said after Cameron explained the situation.

Cameron showed them the labs and hospital facilities, and they immediately took off their coats, donned smocks and started sterilizing the long unused instruments.

Neal Kelso, the linguist, was the last to arrive. In his late twenties, Cameron guessed. Thinning hair, a high forehead, and an intense, preoccupied look in his eyes. He had brought two suitcases full of books, and he stared silently at the spacecraft for two full minutes before he finally spoke.

"My God, let's get going," he said. "Let's get a look inside that thing!"

By mid-afternoon they were all settled in. The equipment had been tested by the engineers and technicians, the hospital was ready, and Neal Kelso had set up a library and work area in one of the lower-floor offices.

"Okay," Harry said when they were all gathered in the conference room. "We'll all be working here until we're ready to issue a report. We'll also be living here. There's a red telephone over there. It's a direct line to General Morrison's office. That will be our only contact with the outside."

Sarah Michaels looked surprised. "That's a bit restrictive, isn't it?"

"Yes," Harry said. "It's meant to be. Until we know exactly what we're dealing with here, this operation is to remain under wraps. I hope it won't be too long."

They all nodded agreement, and Harry took a long breath. "So far, we have detected no radioactivity. Nor have we detected anything else suggesting that the spacecraft poses any danger to us. But we have to be realistic. We have no idea what, or who, might be inside of that thing. There could be elements, or chemicals, or any number of other things that might be harmful, or even deadly to human beings. There is also the possibility that whatever alien beings are in there might regard us as a threat to their lives. If that is so, we can make the assumption that they have weapons . . . weapons that are very probably far superior to anything we know."

There was a silence as Harry glanced around at the solemn faces. He finally smiled. "I'm not trying to frighten anybody. Maybe the thing is empty. But when Paul and Phil and I go out there to look it over, and maybe try to get in, I don't want anybody to be a hero. If we suddenly keel over, or if somebody jumps out of the spacecraft to grab us, don't panic. Okay?"

Everyone nodded.

"All right, let's do it."

They filed out, the technicians going to their monitoring booths overlooking the hangar, Sarah Michaels and Neal Kelso going to one of the lower-floor windows. Cameron and Paul Bannister followed Harry to the air lock door where they pulled on protective suits and helmets with oxygen masks. Cameron was glad he wasn't wearing an astronaut suit with medical-monitoring instruments. The readings from his heart would have shattered the cardiograph machines already. Their helmets were equipped with radio microphones and receivers, and the moment Cameron pulled his on, he could hear Harry's and Paul Bannister's heavy breathing.

Five minutes later, Harry smiled through his plastic face-piece and reached for the air lock door. "Good luck," he said.

The floodlight in the rafters was on, and the row of amber lights at the base of the spacecraft continued to blink. Earlier, Cameron had noted that the amber lights blinked at the same rate as his heartbeat. Now his heart was going twice as fast.

Harry moved ten paces into the hangar and paused, Bannister and Cameron two paces behind. Then he moved forward again, more slowly now. They were moving to within fifty feet of the craft.

"Readings on the magnetometer are rising," one of the technicians said.

Harry turned and looked at the two men behind him, then up at the viewing windows. There were a dozen technicians watching them.

"We trigger some sort of force field?" Cameron asked.

"Possibly," Harry answered. "What are the other readings?"

"All normal," a technician answered.

Harry moved forward to within five feet of the spacecraft's base. Then he turned and moved along the side, slowly circling the beveled skirt.

Cameron followed him closely, studying one of the modules high above them. There were flared openings on one side of it. "Could be propulsion jets," he said.

Harry nodded and moved on. He stopped suddenly and took a step back. "Look at this."

He was pointing to a small, burnlike mark where the base touched the floor. "Could have been made when the satellite hit it," he said.

"Well, that didn't bring it down," Cameron said, "that's for sure." The satellite must have struck with a fairly heavy impact. But there was no sign of a dent in the skin of the structure.

They completed the circle, returning to the facing side. If there was a door anywhere, it seemed likely it would be here. In the recessed area between two of the modules there was a molded framework that normally would suggest a hatch or door of some kind. But within it, the wall was solid black. All three of them stared at the area.

"Question," Bannister said. "How do we open it?"

Cameron gave an uneasy laugh. "Another question . . . Do we want to?"

As quickly as he spoke, all three of the men stiffened. A soft whine was suddenly coming from the spacecraft, like the sound of an electric motor. A moment later, the door of the hatch began to slide upward, exposing an intensely lit area inside the ship. The light seemed almost luminescent.

It took a moment for them to realize why the light was so strange. Then thick clouds of white vapor began pouring out of the hatch, completely obscuring the opening. All three of them stepped back, too startled to speak.

"No negative readings on atmosphere," one of the technicians said quickly, as if to reassure them.

They were not particularly reassured. Whatever the vapor contained, it could very easily be something unknown to the technician's poison detector.

The heavy fog seemed to cling to the sides of the modules for a minute. Then it slowly began to dissolve. Like heavy steam condensing.

"Harry!" Cameron said and pointed to the base of the ship directly in front of them. The whining had started again. A small door was opening in the three-foot-high base. When the door was horizontal, it stopped moving and seemed to click quietly into place. A louder whine followed. Then a heavy, wedge-shaped ramp came sliding out of the opening. It extended itself about eight feet and then stopped, forming a neat inclined walkway rising to the platformed base of the craft. All three men stared uncertainly at it.

"Some sort of . . . invitation?" Harry murmured.

"Yeah," Cameron answered dubiously, " 'Come

in,' said the spider to the fly." After he spoke, he wondered if people from outer space were as devious as earthlings. Did they take hostages and use them for bargaining purposes too? The extended ramp did seem to be an invitation. But an invitation to what?

The vapor was all gone now. Inside the door, the intense light revealed nothing more than a greenish black panel, or bulkhead, eight or ten feet back from the door.

Through his earphones, Cameron heard someone, either Harry or Bannister, take a deep, fortifying breath. He looked at both of them. "Well?"

Harry nodded, his voice thick. "Let's go."

Cameron moved toward the ramp with him. "Who's idea was this?" he asked. The attempt at levity did nothing to relieve his tension.

They moved cautiously up the ramp, to a position between the two modules. Then Harry motioned them to wait as he stepped forward and moved through the door.

Two steps inside the door, Harry paused and quickly looked around, expecting the worst: a man, an animal, some kind of creature poised to defend itself, or to attack. He saw nothing that appeared to be alive. Nor did anything move.

The chamber was ten or twelve feet square, everything in it glistening black. At each of the four corners, a passageway seemed to lead into smaller chambers within the four modules. Harry looked back and motioned for the others to come in.

Cameron and Bannister moved cautiously inside. Then Bannister followed Harry to the right, both of them looking into one of the rooms. "Looks like crew's quarters," Bannister said.

"And you don't have crew's quarters without a crew," Harry answered.

Cameron peered into one of the rooms on the left. It was about the size of a small den. But the only furniture was a hard chair with a three-foot pedestal standing next to it. On top of the pedestal were four buttons, apparently control switches for the blank screen mounted on the wall in front of the chair. The adjacent wall was a mass of closed cubicles, each with a playing-card-sized panel in front. The panels were labelled with different gold symbols, probably indicating the contents of the cubicle. An interesting puzzle for Neal Kelso. Cameron turned back to the central chamber where Harry and Bannister were moving cautiously toward one of the other rooms.

It happened at the same instant Cameron turned. The passageway in front of Harry and Bannister was empty as Cameron turned and glanced in that direction. Then, in a lightning-fast movement, a man suddenly appeared, his body filling the entire doorway. Cameron jumped, every nerve in his body clanging as he gaped at the figure.

Paul Bannister fell back as if struck, and Harry's gasp came clearly through the microphone. The figure seemed huge, the arms partially lifted and flaring out at the sides, both of his feet at least ten inches above the floor!

Harry was the first to recover. "Oh, my God," he groaned. He let out a long sigh and shook his head. "It's a space suit! I must have touched something."

Cameron could see it now. Some kind of a wardrobe door had flown open and blocked the doorway. The space suit was hanging from the door, the legs dangling ten inches above the floor. The suit was empty.

Paul Bannister let out a sigh and leaned heavily against a fluted wall, his eyes shut. Harry glanced at Cameron, a sick smile on his face.

"Well, at least it tells us something," Bannister finally said. "Whoever was operating this thing has got two arms and two legs."

It was true, Cameron realized. The space suit looked as if it would fit a man about six feet tall. But he wasn't sure if that was particularly comforting. His heart was still pounding. "So where is the guy?" he asked.

Bannister glanced around with an uneasy laugh. "You guys mind if I wait in the car?"

One of the technicians suddenly broke in, his voice concerned. "Hey . . . you guys okay?"

"We're fine, Nick," Harry answered. "Nobody here so far." He looked up at the onyx-black ceiling, searching the corners. "There's an upper deck. But how do we get to it?"

All three of them moved to another of the small side chambers. Inside, a chair stood in front of banks of strange-looking, computerlike instruments. Above the instruments were several blank screens.

"Engine room?" Harry suggested.

The symbols on the instruments were very much like those Cameron had seen in the first room. They appeared to be some kind of cuneiform writing. "There must be more than one person to operate all this," Cameron said.

Harry shook his head, unwilling to make any premature guesses. Whether there had been one person or a dozen, at least one of them still had to be on the ship somewhere. He moved back to the central chamber, skirting around the side, glancing once again at the ceiling. "There's got to be a way to get up there."

Cameron moved cautiously around to the opposite side, also studying the ceiling. Then he turned abruptly and stepped back from the wall. A humming sound was suddenly coming from somewhere in the wall, or from the floor beneath it. Harry and Bannister heard it too. They all stood perfectly still, all staring at the floor as a portion of it broke away and began to rise.

It was an elevator! It was rising steadily toward the ceiling. At the same time a portion of the ceiling slid away, providing an opening for the rising platform. When the platform reached the top, there was a soft click and the humming stopped.

Then Cameron saw it: the small floor-plate he

must have stepped on to activate the switches. He touched his foot to the plate again. The humming sound resumed; the elevator slid quietly downward to its former position, and the ceiling panel moved back into place. Cameron looked at the others.

Harry lifted his head and gazed silently at the ceiling. Were the pilots of this thing waiting for them up there? Cowering in fear? Or waiting with weapons? He took a deep breath and moved to the elevator platform.

Bannister moved to Harry's side. "Touch it again," Harry said.

Cameron moved his boot to the plate. Once again the platform hummed and moved upward.

The room above them was dark. After the dazzling lights below, neither of them could see anything more than looming shadows as they rose into the chamber. The platform lifted them to their full height, then clicked into place under their feet.

To their left, soft green lights illuminated banks of instruments and scanners. Neither of them moved as they looked around the chamber, their eyes gradually becoming accustomed to the darkness. Then Harry nudged Bannister and they stepped away from the platform. As quickly as they moved, the elevator clicked and hummed downward. A few seconds later Phil Cameron's head was rising through the hole.

The elevator mechanism clicked off, and for a half-minute they all stood in silence. Then they moved forward toward the glowing controls.

In front of the control panels, there were two couch-chairs similar to those used in capsules and space shuttles. Harry moved to the right of them, Cameron and Bannister to the left. When they were astride the chairs, all three men froze, gaping at the two seated figures.

"Holy God!" Harry breathed.

They were humans . . . or something very close to humans. Their eyes were open, one of them staring at the glowing instruments in front of his knees. The other's head was resting back on the cushioned chair, mouth open, his eyes fixed on a slowly turning scanner at the top of the instrument panel.

They seemed to be alive. But neither man was breathing. Nor was there any evidence of pulsing arteries in their necks. Harry moved closer, reaching out. He touched the wrist of the man on the right. The arm dropped limply from its resting place and dangled at the side.

"Dead," Harry said.

There was still something frightening about the two figures. They were dressed alike in what appeared to be some kind of black military uniforms. The fabric was heavy, with collars rising high around the backs of their necks. On their shoulders were epaulets an inch thick, with some kind of insignia on top, and their waists and hips were tightly encased in some kind of shiny, leatherlike material. Flaring out from their wrists were stiff winglike extensions of material—like exaggerated gauntlets.

But it was their faces that seemed more menacing than anything else. Their heads were completely bald, and they appeared to have no hair other than eyebrows. But their expressions were cold and emotionless. There were no creases or wrinkles around the eyes that might suggest humor or any kind of compassion. And they both wore a slight frown, as if in hard concentration.

Harry looked solemnly at Bannister and Cameron, then cleared his throat. "We've found them," he said into his microphone.

"They're both dead."

VII

It was impossible to get to the Crown Mountain tracking station by airplane or helicopter. That meant they had to fly to Albuquerque, rent a small plane to fly to Gunnison, Colorado, and then rent a car for the two-hour drive into the Rocky Mountains.

Lew Price had called first, establishing that they had tracked the shuttle flight, and that they still had a tape of it. When they arrived at the ten-thousand-foot-altitude, the sky was overcast, and bits of snow were beginning to splatter their windshield. George Turner was a big, bull-sized man with an easy smile and a relaxed manner. When he played linebacker for Northwestern University, the team had the distinguishing record of having lost more football games than any team in Big Ten history.

He got Price and Bancroft mugs of hot coffee, then took them to a small room where he had the radar tapes already threaded into a monitor. "This is what I presume you're looking for," he said and pressed the replay button.

The first blip was in the upper left portion of the screen. "That's you guys in your Orbiter," he said.

"What's the time?" Lew asked.

"Thirty-one hours, ten minutes, ten seconds," Turner answered.

Bancroft started counting aloud. ". . . twelve, thirteen, fourteen, fifteen, and . . . there!"

Turner sipped some coffee and nodded. "And that's your visitor."

The second blip moved across the screen and paused for a minute next to the first blip. Four seconds later, there was a slight bulge, and tiny white bits scattered in all directions. Then the UFO blip moved off toward the bottom of the screen at a thirty degree angle.

"George," Lew asked, after they watched it a second time, "can you project where that thing might've come down?"

"Sure. We followed it all the way to the bottom." He put a second tape into the machine and pushed the fast-forward button. The tape reels whirled and the blip danced wildly around the screen. When he pressed the next button, the blip stopped, then became successively larger as Turner adjusted more controls. "There you are. That's the end of its flight. Bannon County, Arizona." He pulled a road map from his pocket, a small X already marked on it. "Somewhere in that area," he said. "Plus or minus two or three miles."

Bancroft took the map and glanced at the tape machine. "George, what's the chance of borrowing this tape? Or getting a copy made."

Turner put his cup down. He leaned back against a desk and smiled. "You kiddin'? This is a Department of Defense operation. You couldn't walk out of here with that coffee cup."

Lew glanced covetously at the tape. But he couldn't ask George Turner to risk his job—or maybe even a charge of espionage. "Look," he said, "we may need to get back to you later on this."

Turner nodded doubtfully. "This is just a favor, you know. If the brass knew about this, I could get canned just for having you guys in here." He gave them a smile that clearly said please don't press it.

Harry Forbes had experienced a great feeling of relief in finding that the two alien space men posed no physical threat to any of his staff. But the feeling was mixed with regret. There were so many things the two men could have told them—things that might take weeks or months to find out. Or things that might never be learned.

The bodies had been removed and taken to the hangar's small hospital, and Paul Bannister had given the upper flight deck a thorough check for radiation or bacterial contamination. Apparently there was nothing harmful in the environment. So what had caused the aliens to die?

If the cause was not too complex, and if the aliens died for the same reasons human beings died, Sarah Michaels might be able to come up with an answer in an autopsy. But the mysteries of how the spacecraft flew, where it had come from, and what it was doing here still remained. Were the aliens friendly? Unfriendly? Was this their first trip to earth? Or had they been coming around for years? Were the hundreds of flying saucer stories people had been telling in the past thirty or forty years all true? If so, why hadn't the aliens made any effort to communicate directly with the people on earth? Were they frightened of us? Or were they so advanced they considered us a backward form of life that was not worth communicating with?

All kinds of questions assaulted Harry as he came down the elevator and stood in the central chamber below. There were so many he hardly knew where to start in looking for answers. He moved off to the right and into one of the smaller rooms that appeared to be some kind of a laboratory.

Along one side was a counter that looked like it might serve as a workbench. Behind it were small compartmented shelves containing vials and jars and an assortment of instruments. Moving into the room, he felt a crunching under his boot. He quickly stepped back. Two broken vials were lying on the floor. His boot had crushed part of the glass, but it was clear that the vials had been broken before he had entered the room.

He moved cautiously around the shattered pieces and looked at the opposite side of the chamber. A number of glass-faced compartments ran the length of the wall, each with a small button beneath it. In the darkness behind the glass, nothing was visible. He reached forward and tentatively pressed the button closest to the doorway. From somewhere inside the compartment a light snapped on, revealing a collection of various birds and animals and insects. Swirling gently through the entire compartment was a hazy vapor, making it difficult to see the specimens. But they were all recognizable species, apparently samples collected from earth. Was it possible the aliens were biologists? Entymologists?

He moved to the next compartment, a much larger chamber than the others. He pressed the button, expecting to see more birds and reptiles, or perhaps some larger animals. Instead, his heart jumped to his throat and he stared incredulously.

"Holy God!" he breathed.

Inside the chamber, a young woman—a human being—was stretched out on a low table, her eyes closed, her blonde hair stirring gently with the swirl of surrounding vapors.

Harry quickly pulled his walkie-talkie from a back pocket. "Paul! Get in here fast! Bring a gurney!"

Could she possibly be alive? Harry quickly felt around the edges of the glass, searching for some kind of a clasp or lock. At the top he found a small release button. The glass slid downward, leaving the entire chamber open. Harry held his breath against the vapors and grabbed the girl's hand.

It was icy. But there seemed to be some warmth in her face. He slid one arm under her shoulders, the other under her legs and eased her out of the chamber.

"Oh, my God," Bannister gasped as he came into the room.

Harry moved through the door and placed the girl on the gurney Bannister had brought into the central

76

chamber. "I think she's still alive," he said. Bannister frowned and held her wrist, feeling for a pulse as they rolled her down the ramp and quickly through the air lock doors.

Sarah gaped at the girl as she met them inside the hospital. "In the spacecraft?"

"Along with a hundred other animal specimens," Harry answered.

They quickly went to work on her. Sarah examined her eyes, then got out a hypodermic needle and a small bottle of fluid. Bannister checked her mouth, placed an oxygen mask over her face and then began going over her chest with a stethoscope.

"Phil," Harry said into his walkie-talkie, "there's some kind of vapor in one of those lower rooms. Have somebody check it out, will you? It might be dangerous."

My God, he wondered as he put the walkie-talkie away and stared at the girl. Where had she come from? And how long had she been in the spacecraft? She was a very pretty girl, no more than nineteen or twenty, he guessed.

Had they grabbed her somewhere, on some lonely road late at night? Had she struggled against them? Or did they look enough like human beings that she had no idea who or what they were? She must have been terrified when she found herself inside the craft. Or had they rendered her unconscious from the start, and made it all painless?

Somewhere, at some time, she must have been reported missing. She certainly had parents. Or maybe even a husband. Were they searching for her—certain by now that she had been kidnapped, or murdered?

And somewhere, not too far away from where they picked her up, somebody had probably reported seeing a flying saucer. Harry smiled ruefully to himself. Or maybe they didn't report it. Thoughtful people tended to keep UFO sightings to themselves these days. Senator Stoddard, one of the presidential candidates, had admitted seeing a saucer a couple of months ago and almost knocked himself out of the race.

Paul Bannister had hooked up a bottle of something to the girl's arm. He was watching grimly as Sarah carefully examined the girl's scalp and neck. When she was finished, she returned Bannister's grim look, then shook her head.

"She's alive, Harry. But just barely. She's in a deep coma. I can't find any marks on her indicating trauma. But it could be chemically induced. Possibly those vapors in there. You agree, Paul?"

"Yes. She needs intensive care, Harry. A complete neurological check . . . lab checks of blood and tissue. We just don't have the facilities to handle something like that here. We've got to get her to a good hospital."

"Quickly," Sarah added.

Harry nodded. "Okay, come on. Let's talk to Morrison."

He knew Morrison wasn't going to like it. But no matter what Morrison wanted, the girl's life came first. Phil Cameron joined them in the conference room as Harry called the Pentagon and explained the situation on the speaker phone.

Morrison was silent for a minute, obviously unhappy. "Are you sure you can't treat her there, Dr. Michaels?" he finally asked. "It's going to raise a lot of questions if we take her to a hospital."

"She's got to go to a hospital," Sarah said flatly. "We have no way of making a complete diagnosis here. Even if we could, we probably couldn't treat her properly."

Harry was glad she was so emphatic. There was no way Morrison could dispute her medical advice.

"All right," Morrison finally said, "I'll take care of it."

"Fast, General," Sarah said before he could hang up.

The phone clicked dead, and Sarah looked questioningly at Harry. "Will he do it?" she asked.

"He'll do it," Harry said.

Sarah and Bannister quickly left the room, leaving Harry and Phil Cameron alone. Cameron grimaced. "Too bad. That girl could have been a big help to us if she'd been conscious."

Harry nodded. At least she could have told them how long she had been in the spacecraft. It was even conceivable that she had made a trip to another galaxy.

"She still might recover," he said.

"Let's hope so," Cameron said quietly. "The technicians checked out that vapor. It doesn't seem to be dangerous. I've also got them running some cables into the spacecraft. Maybe we can find out what kind of energy source the thing uses. And Neal Kelso's looking over all those cubbyholes in that room on the lower deck."

"Good," Harry said. "And I want a crew to go over the outside of the ship. See if they can find any external damage we might have missed. Tell 'em to use a microscope if they have to. I don't care how small the damage is. Even a pinhole. I want to know if those men were dead or alive when the ship landed."

"Right."

"And there are a couple of vials in that room where the girl was. Get those analyzed too." Harry sat back and closed his eyes, his hands clasped over his head. "It doesn't make sense, Phil. The satellite rockets obviously didn't do any serious damage. And the two men obviously were not knocked out of their seats by the impact. So why are they dead?"

"Indigestion?"

Harry smiled. "That's not so far-fetched. Did you see any food around?"

"There's a small galley in the room with the sleeping quarters. A lot of tubes and jars and what look like chemicals. I've got Tower and Rohrback checking out some samples."

Harry pulled himself up. "Well, it's not likely, I suppose. Let's get something to eat."

Thirty minutes later, Harry returned to the spacecraft hoping there wouldn't be any more surprises like the one in the specimen room. He took the elevator to the flight deck, marveling once again at the conveniences the two men had. In a NASA ship no weight or energy would be wasted on elevators. There would be nothing more than a ladder, and the astronauts would be lucky to have that.

He sat down on one of the couches where they had found the dead men and stared at the confusing array of controls. With their strange identification symbols, there was no way of knowing what any of them did. He reached across to a button and placed his finger on it, then hesitated. A power button? Something that would send the whole ship rocketing through the roof of the hangar? Somehow the button didn't look important enough for that. He gave it a quick punch.

The reaction startled him. The big screen directly in front of him flashed on, filling the whole room with light. Then he realized the light was coming indirectly from the floodlights of the hangar. Somewhere on the exterior of the ship there must be a TV camera feeding into this screen. He could see across the hangar to the air lock doors and to where the technicians were working behind windows. He pressed the adjacent button.

The picture moved now, the camera apparently turning, showing him a complete three-hundred-and-sixty-degree view of the hangar's interior. When it had returned to its original position, he pressed the first button again. The camera stopped moving.

The ambulance must have arrived outside. Two technicians were helping Sarah and Bannister pull a gurney through the double hospital doors. The girl was covered with blankets now.

God help her, Harry thought. When she woke up, she would probably need all the help she could get.

VIII

The Bannon County Airport was listed in the flight guide, but it looked more like a poorly plowed field with a pair of old pantyhose for a windsock. Tower-control seemed to consist of a man in coveralls who waved at them from the hangar when Lew made a low pass over the place. But a couple of private planes tied down at the north end of the field seemed to indicate it was possible to land without somersaulting. Lew brought the Beechcraft down with both he and Steve holding their breath through the length of the runway.

When they taxied down to the other planes, the man in coveralls arrived on a rickety bicycle, now wearing an old railroad cap. "Howdy," he said.

"How you doin'?" Lew answered.

"What can I do fer ya?" He straddled the bike and leaned on the handlebars, giving them a toothless grin.

"We're looking for a place to tie down for a while," Steve told him.

"Jest leave her set right where she is. Yer the first plane landed here this week. Ain't gonna block nobody."

"Great," Steve said. "Thanks."

The man smiled and held out his hand. "That's ten a day. First ten in advance."

Steve paid him, and they set about securing the lines. "Do you have a car we could rent?"

"Nope."

Lew groaned and looked past the hangar. There didn't appear to be any civilization within ten miles. "We need some way to get around. Do you know of any place we could rent something?"

"Yep."

"Where?"

"From me."

Steve wondered if they had landed in Vermont by mistake. "I thought you said you didn't have a car we could rent."

The man chuckled over his little joke. "Don't," he said. "Got a pickup truck. You didn't ask me about a truck. You asked me about a car. Ain't got no car."

"A truck'll be fine."

The man nodded. "It's 'round t'other side of the hangar. Keys are in it." He lifted his palm again. "Twenty a day."

They both dug in their pockets this time. The man folded the bills neatly and stuffed them into a frayed wallet. "Buy yer own gas, 'course. I ain't no millionaire."

"By chance, you heard anything about a crash in this area the last couple days?" Steve asked.

The man grinned as if they were a couple more in a long line of idiots he had confronted lately. "You must be talkin' about that crazy story Sam Tate was tellin'. Dragged the sheriff out there and everything." He gave a cackling laugh. "Said he saw some kinda big airplane thing come down. Like a flyin' saucer . . . you know, like on the TV."

"Where was this?" Lew asked.

"Shoot, I don't know. You'll have to ask the sheriff." He grinned again. "See, it's the desert air does it. Dries up all yer brain juice so's ya can't think straight no more. Happens to everybody out here."

Steve glanced at Lew. "Maybe we ought to talk with the sheriff."

Lew nodded. "Can you tell us where we can find the sheriff?"

"Right in the middle of town, back of the court-house."

"Thanks."

"If that pickup don't start," the man called after them, "ain't no refunds."

Sheriff Barlow didn't appear to be a man whose brain juices had dried up. He looked like a cop who'd seen enough thieves and drunks and murderers that he wasn't too surprised by anything any more. He lounged back in his chair and nodded. Yes, he knew Sam Tate, and Sam had reported everything to him yesterday morning.

"I went out there with him," Barlow said patiently. "And I found exactly what I expected to find. Nothin'." He took a long breath and shrugged. "It ain't that Sam deliberately lies. It's just the way he is. You take him or leave him." He gave a short laugh. "Even called Washington. I don't know where he got the money, but he must've made five calls to Herb Pope. Herb's our congressman."

Steve wondered what the sheriff would say if they told him about the radar tapes. But there wasn't any more reason for the sheriff to believe the tapes than there was for him to believe Sam Tate. "Where can we find Tate?" he asked.

Barlow shrugged. "I dunno."

"Doesn't he have a home? Or some place he hangs out?"

"Well, Sam's a drifter. Comes and goes. Ambles off looking for work, then comes back and nests some-where till he needs a job again."

"So you think he's left town?"

"Probably. He was working for Charlie Keller up till yesterday noon. He didn't come back after lunch-time, and he didn't show up last night at the trailer court where he lives. That's pretty much his usual pattern. He could be up in Utah, or headed for Oregon by now."

"Can you tell us where he claims to have seen the saucer?"

"Sure. Just go right out in front of the courthouse and follow that road to the east. Six or eight miles out you'll see Pete's Polish Palace. Couple miles after that you'll see a dirt road on the left. Follow that up a hill till it reaches a saddle. He said he saw the saucer off to the right in a little shallow place."

They rose to go. "Thanks a lot, Sheriff."

"You want some good advice?" Barlow asked.

They knew what was coming—a few words of wisdom about how not to make a fool of yourself. "Sure," Lew said.

The advice was better than that. "If I was you," Barlow said, and pulled himself slowly out of the chair, "I'd go directly to a gas station from here. The gas gauge in that old clunker Ace Landon rented you don't work. It says 'full,' but Ace generally siphons it down to a couple quarts before he rents it out."

Steve smiled. "Thanks. We appreciate it."

The old clunker, which was a thirty-year-old Ford with bulging fenders and no upholstery on the seats, took sixteen gallons of gas and three quarts of oil. The gas station attendant grinned knowingly as he filled it up. They paid up and finally got headed east.

"Sounds like Mr. Sam Tate was not exactly Bannon County's leading citizen," Lew said, struggling with the gear lever.

Steve nodded, his thoughts elsewhere. "It really doesn't matter. We know the thing came down out here, and Tate's story verifies it. But there's something else that bothers me."

"What?"

"If they followed that saucer down at Crown Mountain, we can be damned certain that Norad followed it down too."

"So?"

"So why all the hocus pocus? Why is someone

erasing tapes and trying to pretend the thing never existed? It doesn't make any sense. And where did Harry go on a 'secret' assignment? Did you ever hear of anyone in NASA going on a secret assignment?"

"Not lately," Lew answered. He squinted at the road ahead. "Here comes Pete's Polish Palace."

They rattled past, and Lew looked closely at the odometer. It wasn't working.

It didn't matter. Three minutes later the dirt road showed up on the left, and there was a low hill in the distance. Lew slowed the truck and swung it off the highway, bouncing heavily into the deep ruts. The road gradually rose and curved upward around the hill. When they reached the saddle, Lew hit the brakes and slid to a stop.

"Barlow said it was a shallow place off to the right."

"Probably just past that rise," Steve answered. He pushed the door open. "Let's take a look."

They angled around the hill, then dropped past the rise. The shallow clearing was about two hundred feet across, a bed of sand and rocks with a few tufts of dried grass. Barlow was right. There certainly was no saucer there now. They moved toward the center, kicking aimlessly at the rocks.

Lew suddenly stuck out a hand, then pointed. "Hey . . . hold it. Look at that! You ever see any animal tracks that looked like that?"

The area ahead of them was covered with parallel grooves, obviously made by the teeth of a rake. Or more likely by a dozen rakes. The teeth marks covered an area forty or fifty feet square.

"Someone is trying to hide something," Lew said.

Steve nodded. "And it looks like a very thorough job."

They moved forward again, kicking aside the raked sand. "Look at this," Steve said. "The sand below is all darker. It's been burned." He knelt and dug out an odd-shaped rock. It looked like a couple of lumpy baseballs pressed together. The composition of the two rocks was obviously different.

"Huh," Lew grunted and ran a hand over them. "It'd take the heat of a blast furnace to fuse this together."

"Or a rocket of some kind," Steve said and moved on.

"Steve?" Lew said in a hushed voice.

Steve glanced back at him. Lew was squinting up at the saddle where they had left the truck. Forty yards beyond the truck, and partially hidden by a clump of brush, was a black sedan. Standing close to it were two men in business suits. The taller man was watching them through a pair of binoculars.

"I've seen that car before," Lew said. "Out by the airport. It was parked at the side of the road with those same two guys sitting in it."

"You sure?"

"They were wearing business suits. And I haven't noticed a whole lot of businessmen in this area."

Steve nodded and resumed kicking at the sand, keeping an eye on the two men. "Let's see how big an area this burned spot covers."

"They're coming," Lew said.

The men had returned the binoculars to the car and were moving slowly down the slope. They didn't seem to be in any hurry. And there was nothing menacing in their appearance. They looked like a couple of easterners out for a stroll on the desert.

"Morning," the shorter one said. He was smiling, glancing from Steve to Lew.

"Hi," Lew answered.

"What can we do for you?" Steve asked.

"This is private property," the tall man said. "Flat Butte Mining."

"So?"

"So you're trespassing."

"Sorry," Steve said amiably. The two men had

separated, as if to outflank them. Their smiles were not so friendly now.

The short man nodded at the rock in Steve's hand. "What have you got there?"

"This? It's . . . it's for my kid. He's got a rock collection."

"Well, we're starting an exploratory operation here. You'll have to leave that." The man moved forward, his hand out.

Lew smiled and stepped closer to Steve, intercepting the man. "We're not trying to jump your claim, if that's what you're worried about."

"Then there's no reason not to give it to me, is there?" He moved forward again, brushing past Lew, this time determined.

"I guess not," Steve said. When the man was almost to him, he tossed the rock a couple of feet in the air. The action accomplished exactly what he hoped it would. The man's head lifted and he stepped quickly to the side to catch the rock. Steve slammed his fist into the exposed chin.

Steve's action surprised Lew. But there was no choice now but to go the distance.

He whirled on the taller man, swinging blindly with all his strength. The fist caught the man on the side of the face, sending him sprawling to the ground. It was a devastating blow, and the man was not likely to get up for a minute or two. Lew turned quickly to where the first man was rising from his hands and knees. Steve was moving forward, but from the way he was grimacing and holding his right hand close to his body, it was clear he wasn't going to throw any more right-handed punches. Lew took a quick step forward and drove his foot into the rising man's abdomen. The blow landed squarely, but Lew also landed on his back from the effort. He rolled to his hands and knees, grabbed the rock and scrambled to his feet, running. "Let's get the hell outa here!" he yelled.

Steve was right with him. They took off at full

speed, angling upward, and then straight across the side of the hill. Almost at the truck, Lew eased his stride and looked back.

The taller man was on one knee, both arms out in front of him, holding something. A gun? The second man turned sharply and said something. The taller man immediately lowered his arms.

They piled into the truck and slammed the doors. Lew quickly got the engine going, backed the truck into the brush and swung it around. As they headed down the road, they could see the two men scurrying up the slope. Lew pushed the throttle to the floor, sending the old truck bouncing and banging down the road.

Steve was shaking his hand, blowing on the scuffed knuckles. "I haven't punched out anybody since high school."

"How's your other hand?" Lew asked.

"Why?"

Lew glanced in the rearview mirror. They were almost at the highway now. Behind them, the black car was starting down the hill. "You might need it," Lew said. "I think they still want to talk to us."

"I don't want to talk to them." Steve smiled over at Lew. "Do you want to talk to 'em?"

"Maybe tomorrow," Lew said. "My social calendar is pretty full at the moment." He eased off the throttle, then hit it hard as he swung the wheel to the right and skittered onto the highway. He pushed the pedal to the floorboard and watched in the mirror. Five seconds later the black car came skidding around the corner.

"Who are those guys?!"

Steve was watching through the rear window. The car was coming fast, closing the gap, edging over to the left side of the highway. "They're gonna try to pass."

A big diesel was coming in the opposite direction, its air horn blasting. The black sedan swung in behind the pickup, and the diesel roared past.

Lew had the throttle floored, but the black sedan

swung left and moved easily forward. The tall man was on the passenger side. He rolled down his window and shouted, gesturing for them to pull over. Lew gave them only a glance, and kept the pedal on the floor.

The tall man finally gave up the shouting. The driver pulled a few feet forward and swung his steering wheel hard to the right. The car slammed into the truck's left front fender.

"Jesus!" Lew muttered, and fought to keep the truck on the road. "These guys are crazy!"

The car slammed into them again. Then it eased back. A camper, followed by two cars, was coming toward them, horns blasting. As quickly as they passed, the sedan was back again. This time it pulled well ahead and edged to the right, trying to force them off the road.

"Hang on," Lew said. He eased off and swung to the left. When the sedan moved left to cut him off, he swung right again, jammed the throttle to the floor and bulled his way forward. There was a screech of metal and then the clang of a hubcap bouncing away. But they were through the gap.

Behind them, the sedan swerved left and right, then straightened and resumed the chase. Lew glanced at the mirror, then squinted at the road ahead. A half mile away, a railroad light was blinking. Lew waited until they were fifty yards from it, then easing off the throttle at the last moment, he swung the truck sharply to the right, skidding onto a narrow road that paralleled the tracks. He pushed the pedal to the floor again. Behind them, the sedan skidded through a half revolution and came to a stop facing the other way.

"Oh boy!" Lew gasped; Steve whirled from the back window and looked. Fifty yards ahead of them the narrow road ended. Apparently it was nothing more than a utility road leading to the loading ramp of a small railroad terminal. There was nowhere to go but up the ramp. The loading dock at the end of it was piled high with drums and crates and sacks of fertilizer. "Hold on!" Lew yelled.

Steve grabbed the dashboard with one hand, the back of the seat with the other and lowered his head as they suddenly flew upward. An instant later, empty oil drums and shattered crates were flying in all directions. The truck caromed from one side of the dock to the other. Then they were in the air again.

They hit the ground nose-first, and bounced. Then they were skidding, sliding through a half circle, finally coming to a stop with their rear end jammed into a fence.

Both of them stared at the loading dock, mouths open as they saw the black sedan appear. It came flying up the ramp, drums and crates exploding in all directions. A split second later, it was going off the side, its rear end lifting high in the air. The nose hit hard. Then the car somersaulted completely and slammed into an embankment. It held for a minute, then tumbled slowly down the slope and stopped, its roof straddling the railroad tracks.

The only sound for a minute was the steady dinging of the crossing signal. Then they heard the blast of a diesel engine and the oncoming rumble of a fast-moving freight train.

"Let's get out of here," Steve said. "I'd rather not be around when Sheriff Barlow shows up."

The truck was listing badly to the right, but it still ran. Lew shot forward, maneuvering past the dock and the scattering of drums and crates. A half minute later they were back on the highway.

"You know, those guys were trying to kill us," Lew said.

Steve nodded, massaging his bruised knuckles again. "Somebody is awfully determined to stop us from finding out anything about that saucer."

"Maybe we really should go to the police, Steve."

"You mean Sheriff Barlow? Or would you rather

call the FBI, and have them send out a couple of guys in dark business suits?"

Lew gave him a dark glance. "I see what you mean. Okay, where to?"

Steve reached under the seat and found the fused rock. "All we've got so far is this. Why don't we take it over to Western Tech? There's a guy there we can show it to. Andrew Mills."

"Can we trust him?"

"He's a nice guy. He'll check it out for us. He ran a NASA seminar on astro-geology . . . before you came into the program."

Lew nodded. "You do understand, I'm starting to get a little worried about my health?"

IX

Gordon Cain had the driver park at the far end of the underground garage. Lafferty, he knew, would be waiting near the front. But there was no point in letting his chauffeur witness any more of his clandestine meetings than was necessary. As quickly as the big car squealed to a stop, he stepped out of the back seat, slammed the door and strode briskly along the slick pavement.

The call from General Morrison saying they had found a live human being in the spacecraft had left Cain speechless. That was the last thing he expected—or wanted—to hear. Even worse, it was a young woman in her twenties. So he had risked a call to Lafferty directly from the White House.

Then came the second shock: Lafferty's return call five hours later. "She's dead," the man said simply.

There were four people in Cain's office at the time. He didn't dare ask for details. He hastily arranged another meeting, excused himself and hurried out of the White House. How could the man be so damned stupid?! Or had it been deliberate, he wondered—an attempt to maneuver him into a vulnerable position?

Lafferty was there, waiting in the shadows, barely visible in the poorly lighted garage.

"What the hell do you mean she's dead?" Cain blurted out in a half whisper. "Did you . . . ?"

"Take it easy, Mr. Cain," Lafferty said quietly. "We didn't kill her."

"Then what happened?"

"We got an ambulance out there and picked her up. As quickly as we got out on the highway, she woke up screaming. She was out of her head."

"What do you mean, 'out of her head'? What killed her?"

"I don't know what killed her, Mr. Cain. She was fighting and screaming, trying to get out of the ambulance. Then she suddenly went limp, and . . ." He shrugged. "She was dead."

"Oh, Jesus," Cain sighed. He gave Lafferty a hard look. "Is that the truth?"

"Mr. Cain . . ."

A pair of headlights swung down the ramp and they both turned their heads away. The car parked near the elevator and a man jumped out and disappeared.

"We were taking her to a private hospital where she would have been kept under wraps as long as necessary," Lafferty said. "We had no reason to kill her."

"Okay. So what did you do with the body?"

"Buried it."

"Buried it! You can't just dump a body in a hole out in the middle of nowhere!"

Lafferty gave him a cold look. "Mr. Cain, be realistic. We had an anonymous body on our hands. We don't want anyone to know where it came from. What else could we do?"

Cain stared at him for a minute, then turned to go.

"Mr. Cain?" Lafferty said quietly.

Cain turned back.

"There's something you should keep in mind," Lafferty said. "I didn't call you. You called me."

Cain started to speak, then thought better of it. He strode away, his jaws clenched tight, his anger

93

seething. He hoped to God he wouldn't get any more phone calls from Morrison. At least not for another week and a half.

"The X-rays are interesting," Sarah said. "Their hearts, lungs and other vital organs appear to be identical to ours. Physically, at least. Biologically? . . . We'll have to wait for the lab test."

She was washing her hands, pulling on a pair of surgical gloves as she talked. On the table, one of the aliens was stretched out on his back, arms at his sides, stripped to the waist. Except for his eyebrows, the man seemed to be completely devoid of hair. The skin was smooth and pale, but beneath it the muscles were large and well developed. In a fight, the man would be a powerful adversary.

Harry stood back against the wall, his arms folded, gazing coldly at the cadaver. After what he had found in the specimen room, it was hard to have any sympathy for the man. He looked enough like a human being that it was also hard to believe he could treat that girl the way he had.

"One surprising thing," Sarah said, bringing a tray of instruments to the surgical table, "is that they have an appendix, a tail bone, and a harderian gland behind the eyeball. We have them too. They're useless to us. I don't know about him, but it's obvious that we've both gone through the same evolutionary process. It's startling."

"Why?" Harry asked.

Sarah shrugged. "We tend to think of our own evolutionary process as unique. That we are a product of thousands of years of biological accidents and externally imposed conditions. That a creature from millions of miles away would have the same accidents, and be exposed to the same external conditions, would be rather extraordinary."

"I see what you mean."

Paul Bannister came in, already in his surgical

gown and gloves. He brought a clipboard over to the table, then smiled at Sarah. "Where are you?" he asked.

She was staring solemnly at the alien's face, obviously daydreaming for a moment. "Just wondering about him," she said. "Who he was, . . . what he was, . . . where he came from, . . . what his world was like. Did he have a wife . . . a family?"

Bannister gave a short laugh. "If he did, he probably kept them in a jar. Or in a smoky specimen chamber."

Sarah gave him a wan smile and picked up a scalpel. She quickly made three long incisions in the shape of a Y. The bloodless flesh opened smoothly, and Sarah reached for more instruments. Harry quickly turned away and left the room.

He poured himself a cup of coffee, then stood at one of the windows overlooking the hangar. Four technicians were giving the lower part of the spacecraft a close inspection, wiping the surface with a cloth, touching it, peering close in an effort to spot any damage.

Harry was beginning to feel that his first reaction to the ship and its occupants might be more accurate than ever. There was something ominous about its dark, brutal appearance. There were no guns apparent, but it still reminded him of some ancient, warlike contraption. It seemed like it should clank and rattle and move ponderously across muddy, World War I trenches, spewing smoke and flames in all directions. It was hard to believe that it darted through space like a super-charged hummingbird.

He emptied his cup and placed it on a desk. Then he caught his breath, listening. One of the technicians sitting at a computer console also heard it. His head lifted sharply and he stared through the window at the spacecraft.

It was a low, growling sound that seemed to vibrate through the floor and send a rumbling through the whole building. In the hangar, the four men who were inspecting the hull of the ship suddenly jumped away. Then they turned and ran.

"Holy Christ!" the man next to Harry cried out. He came abruptly to his feet.

One edge of the spacecraft was rising from the floor. From below it came a blinding white glow, and a steady blast of air was throwing up dust and debris. The roar was deafening, even from behind the glass.

Harry whirled and ran from the room. He burst through the air lock doors and came to an abrupt halt inside the hangar. The entire spacecraft was now two feet above the floor, tilting one way and then the other, as if attempting to balance itself. Harry gaped at it, his heart pounding. Then he glanced at the overhead girders, expecting the thing to burst through them at any moment.

Instead, the roar suddenly stopped. The light beneath the ship gradually faded; at the same time, the craft silently eased itself back down to the floor.

Harry sprinted up the ramp and inside the central chamber. Neal Kelso was standing in the passageway to one of the small rooms, his face white. "What happened?" he asked.

Harry shook his head and took the elevator, his heart still pounding. On the flight deck, Phil Cameron and a technician were standing at a control panel, both of them looking as frightened as everybody else had been.

"What the devil happened?" Harry demanded.

Cameron shook his head. "We just pulled out that tray of electronics. We had it over there looking at it, when . . ." He smiled sheepishly. "When we turned back, the control panel was lit up like a Christmas tree and we were going up."

Harry let out a heavy sigh. "Well, watch what you're doing!"

Cameron nodded, then glanced irritably across the cabin. "Harry, if we're going to find out anything here, we can't keep our hands in our pockets. We've gotta do something."

It was true, Harry realized. But he wasn't sure if his heart could take any more such surprises. "You're right, Phil. I'm sorry. What did the electronics tray look like?"

The technician smiled. "It didn't look like anything they bought at Radio Shack, that's for sure."

"I don't know," Cameron said. "But at least we know how to get this thing going. It's a starting point. Maybe we can trace things down from there and find some clues about what makes it go."

Neal Kelso had come up the elevator, the color back in his face now. "Can I show you something downstairs, Harry?"

Harry smiled. "If you promise not to send me into orbit."

"It's a kind of library," Kelso said when they moved into the small room below. "Apparently those characters on each of the cubbyholes designate the contents. Except you can't open the cubbyholes."

The cubbyholes covered an entire wall of the room, between two and three hundred of them. The characters labeling them were configurations of circles and dots and wedge-shaped marks. Beneath each label was a red button. "What do the buttons do?" Harry asked.

Kelso smiled. "Watch." He pressed one of the buttons. On the wall to their right, a large screen immediately lighted, displaying the same character as on the cubbyhole. Kelso sat down on a chair in front of the screen and manipulated the control button on a low pedestal. The character on the screen shrank almost to nothing. Then it expanded and went in and out of focus. Kelso pressed another control button and a mass of characters appeared.

"It's like pages of a book," Kelso said. "Apparently the symbol designates the subject matter, and there are hundreds, maybe thousands of pages of text for each subject."

"Wonderful," Harry said dryly. "So what do the books say?"

Kelso was frowning as the screen, too absorbed in his own thoughts to note Harry's light sarcasm. "It's curious how much these characters resemble some of the cuneiform inscriptions of the Sumerians. Notice how so many of the marks are wedge-shaped."

It was true. Some of the characters were no more than two intersecting wedges. Others were triangles or squares made up of wedges. The curved lines were also like crescents or quarter moons, and none of the figures had simple, even lines.

"The theory is that the cuneiform writing developed over hundreds, or perhaps thousands of years," Kelso said. "And the characteristic wedge shape came from the fact that the people originally wrote on clay tablets. But it is hard to make a clean line on soft clay. So the person making the tablet would thrust the stylus into the clay and then extend the mark. That's what made the wedge shape. And hence the name *cuneiform*. In Latin, the word *cuneatus,* or *cuneus,* means wedge."

Harry nodded. "So?"

"So it's curious that these people should also have so many wedges. Did they also start out with clay tablets? And if so, why didn't they develop cleaner characters, as we did? It also appears as though they do not have an alphabet system as most civilized cultures have. Theirs seems to be more like a Chinese or Japanese system—something evolved from ideograms, with a different symbol for every word. The alphabet, or letter-sound system, is obviously better. So we have to wonder why they didn't develop something on that order.

"There's the possibility, of course," he went on, "that their brains are so superior to ours that they never felt a need for an alphabet. Maybe they could glimpse thousands of symbols like these and easily retain the memory of them."

"Neal," Harry said, "speculations about the origins of their language are all very interesting. But for the present, is there any way you can decipher it?"

Kelso was still squinting thoughtfully at one of the projected "pages." "It's all tied together, Harry. The origins might give us the key to deciphering it." He switched off the screen and looked at the bank of cubbyholes. "I'm going to bring a computer in here. Then go eeny, meenie, miney, mo, hook it up to one of these books and see what happens."

Harry nodded. "Okay. I'll check back in a couple hours and see what you've got."

Kelso turned sharply as Harry moved toward the door. "Harry . . . it's taken experts two thousand years to translate the Etruscan."

"Oh?" Harry said. "In that case, you'd better take a short lunch."

Phil Cameron and the technician were coming down the elevator carrying a small electronic tray when Harry moved back into the central chamber. "We bypassed the power cables and got this thing out," Cameron said. "We're going to take it into the computers and see what they can tell us about it."

"You're sure this thing won't take off?" Harry asked.

Cameron smiled and disappeared through the door.

Harry returned to the flight deck by the elevator. He eased down on one of the couches and gazed at the array of controls and instruments, wondering what thoughts the two dead space travelers had when they sat here. They had a collection of specimens from earth, including a human being. Were they on their way home when the satellite hit them? Or was it conceivable that they had already been home with the specimens and they were bringing them back to earth? Not likely, he decided. No matter how much regard they might have had for the girl's life, they certainly wouldn't have bothered bringing a collection of lizards and butterflies back to their homes.

He reached forward and pushed the same button he had pressed earlier. Above it, the screen brightened and he could see Phil Cameron and three technicians working at a computer, making attachments to the electronic tray they had taken from the ship. He took a breath, held it for a minute, and pressed a second button.

Cameron and the technicians faded out and a strange symbol took their place. It was in the general shape of a square, with three triangular forms at the top, and a small, tilted rectangle at the bottom. In the center were three circles, the outer one broken at the bottom.

The symbol abruptly disappeared and was replaced by a picture of three soldiers in battle gear running across a clearing. All three of them dropped to the ground, and the sound of automatic rifle fire suddenly rattled through a speaker. The picture then disappeared, instantly replaced by six B-52 bombers flying with their bomb-bay doors open. Strings of bombs came pouring out. Then the picture shifted to the ground where the bombs were exploding across what looked like a Vietnamese village. The sound reverberated through the flight deck of the spacecraft. Then a helicopter gunship was making a low pass over a jungle, all guns firing.

Harry gaped at the screen, even more startled by the next series of pictures. They were brief clips, none of them lasting more than four or five seconds: crowded cities, subways, freeways, rockets blasting off, big commercial jets landing, private planes, factories, mines, mills, rock concerts. All of it was accompanied by a tangle of noise: police calls, aircraft transmissions, newscasts, music—popular, classical, disco, rock, jazz . . .

"Okay, old buddy . . ." the drawling voice of a

disc jockey said, "stack them eights . . ." Then over-lapped by other voices, "Two-Mary-Four, Two-Mary-Four . . . The weather for New York and vicinity, . . . Now the top of the Top Forty, . . . You're cleared for take-off, Delta, . . . President Duncan Tyler declared today that, . . . Nine-eleven Elm Drive. See the man . . . The House today passed and sent to the Senate . . ."

The same tangled series of pictures then shifted to foreign countries and foreign languages, all of it equally noisy.

"It seems to be a tape of broadcasts," Neal Kelso said from behind Harry. He was coming across from the elevator, gaping at the pictures. "They must have been monitoring them."

"Yeah," Harry said. He was searching for something that might lower the volume. Before he could find the right knob or button, the sound faded and the symbol came back on.

"What's that?" Kelso asked.

Harry shook his head. "I don't know. It was at the beginning, too."

"I've seen it before, Harry. I'm sure of it. It's on one of those cubbyholes down in the library."

"What's it mean?"

"I don't know, but I'll take a guess. All the other 'books' have what seems to be written titles. But this one's a symbol."

"For what?"

"The earth. It's got to be, Harry. Everything on that film, or tape, or whatever it is, is a scene from earth. It's sort of an impressionistic overview of everything on earth."

Harry nodded, wondering if it were really a fair depiction of the activities on this planet. There were a lot of good things going on on earth that were very quiet, or even silent. But it would have been hard for them to see inside of churches, or universities, or even in people's homes.

"It reminds me of something, Harry," Kelso said thoughtfully. He headed for the elevator. "I'm going to check with research."

Harry watched him go, then turned back to the controls. He didn't particularly want to watch any more home movies. But did he dare touch any of the other buttons? Phil Cameron had taken the electronics out of the power console. So it seemed safe. He pressed the button activating the external camera. Once again he saw the men outside the ship, and the technicians working behind the window. Then he gazed once more at the control panel. In the center, a large green button had lighted up when he activated the camera. Around the outside of the button was a series of markings, with a small pointer. Harry turned the pointer up to the first marking. Nothing happened. He looked at the screen again, then depressed the button. Then he gasped and pulled his finger back.

Everything had trembled for an instant. But worse than that, a dazzling white light had streaked across the viewing screen. It had raced past two of the technicians and continued straight through the wall of the hangar. There was now a gaping three-foot hole in the wall, and the metal around the hole was molten white and smoking.

"Oh, my God," Harry breathed. He quickly jumped from the couch and bounded across to the elevator. The button had activated some kind of heat ray, or laser beam, he realized as the platform took him down.

When he reached the outside of the spacecraft, the two technicians were staring angrily at him, and Phil Cameron was coming hurriedly through the air lock doors.

"Everyone all right?" Harry asked.

The technicians nodded uncertainly, but Cameron's face was flushed with anger. "What happened?" he demanded.

Harry gave him a sheepish glance. "I should have kept my hands in my pockets."

"Look at this place," Cameron exclaimed.

Harry hadn't seen it on the viewing screen, but one of the computers the technicians had been working with at the side of the spacecraft was now a small pile of smoldering junk. Beyond it, the center of a long wooden table was gone. The two ends were now resting on the floor, a small scattering of charred wood between them.

Harry shook his head in wonder. "And I had it set at the bottom of the dial."

X

The Western Institute of Technology was not as old, nor as prestigious, as Cal Tech, or M.I.T., but the students had that same faraway look in their eyes. They all carried fancy calculators and stacks of incomprehensible books, and they shuffled across the campus as if unaware of anything or anybody around them. Steve and Lew got directions to the geology building from a girl in the admissions office, and they found Andrew Mills in a cluttered cubbyhole on the third floor. He was a small man in his sixties wearing a threadbare sweater under a corduroy jacket.

Steve had called him from the Bannon County Airport, and the professor had promised to wait in his office for them. When they arrived, Mills cleared a place on an old couch for them to sit, and Steve outlined their story, including all the cover-up efforts. Then he handed over the rock.

The professor didn't seem impressed. He turned the rock over a couple of times and studied it through his bifocals. Then he placed it on the desk, sat back with his hands folded across his stomach and regarded the ceiling for a minute. "I appreciate the situation you find yourselves in," he said in a weary, professorial voice. "But let's take your premise. Let us suppose the government actually has a crashed saucer in their hands. Do you really think they'd tell anybody? It doesn't really seem likely, does it?"

"But why keep it from us?" Steve asked. "Lew and I both have security clearances."

Mills smiled. "Security clearance from whom? NASA? Do you have security clearance from the Air Force? Or the CIA? The FBI? You underestimate the paranoia of the United States Government. Or the even deeper paranoia between the various branches and agencies of the government."

"But it doesn't make any sense," Lew said.

"Of course it doesn't. But making sense is rarely a criteria for acceptable bureaucratic behavior. From the government's point of view it's a complicated proposition. Let me ask you . . . What do you think the reaction of the American public would be if they knew the Air Force had a crashed UFO in their possession?"

Lew sighed impatiently. "You'll have to excuse me, but I'm more concerned with *my* reaction to what's going on. We've been chased, almost killed—and the whole country thinks we're responsible for Gates' death."

"Lew, take it easy," Steve cautioned.

Mills was nodding. "I understand your position. How you feel. But it's important that you understand what you're facing—the scope of this thing. It's not some personal vendetta against you and Steve. This is something the government doesn't want the American public to know about. And from what you've said, they're worried enough, or frightened enough, that they'll go as far as necessary to keep it quiet."

"Why?" Lew asked.

"Ahhh . . . *why*? That, of course, is the eternal question when we deal with governments. Why does the CIA experiment with the citizens who employ them? Why does the Congress of the United States not pass a gun control law when the majority of the people want one? Why . . . ?" Mills shrugged.

"So where does that leave us?" Steve asked.

Mills turned his attention back to the rock. "Considering what you have told me, I can see how you feel this rock could be pretty important. Anything we find—high magnetization, irradiation, trace elements that shouldn't be there—anything to give your story some credence."

"How long will it take?" Lew asked.

Mills smiled and picked up the rock. "I'll take it down to the lab before I leave. We should have a report by eleven tomorrow morning."

Harry had not realized how many books Neal Kelso had brought to Texas with him. His office looked like the back room of a used bookstore. There were books on the table, on his desk, and a couple of dozen more still resting in an open suitcase. Harry had wandered in to tell him it was almost dinner time. But Kelso didn't seem interested.

"Look at this, Harry," he said and held a book open on his desk.

It was a picture of a pyramid, one of the Mexican or Mayan structures, with broad steps and some kind of a temple on top. "Mayan?" Harry asked.

"No. Nobody knows who built it. It's called the Pyramid of Tetanapa, and the carbon tests indicate it pre-dates the Mayans by at least two thousand years. And it's bigger than any pyramid in Egypt. At the time of the Spanish Conquest, it was completely covered. No one knew it existed. A Spanish church was built on top of it without anybody knowing what was underneath."

"Why was it covered?"

Kelso shrugged. "Perhaps it was natural growth. Or maybe someone, for some reason, wanted to hide it. Anyway, here's the point. The pyramid is honeycombed with passageways, and those passageways are covered with inscriptions." Kelso quickly turned some pages to where he had a paper marker. "Here's some photographs of those inscriptions. Now compare them with these."

Next to the photographs he placed a sheet of paper with tracings from the symbols and characters in the spacecraft. Harry could see the similarities. The inscriptions from the pyramid were cruder. And none of them were as complex as some of the spacecraft symbols. But the wedge-shaped marks were similar and a few of the configurations were almost identical.

"See what I mean?" Kelso said. "And both of these are similar to the Sumerian. Much too similar to have been an accident. I think they all have the same root. Developed differently, but from the same source."

"So you think there's a connection?"

"There might be. I think it's close enough that the Tetanapa inscriptions might be the key to the translation. I think it's worth a shot, Harry."

Harry nodded, not too certain he understood what Kelso had in mind. At that moment, Phil Cameron came through the door.

"Harry, I've got to talk to you."

"Fine," Harry said and moved toward the door. "Let's all go eat."

Kelso swung around to get more books from the table. "I'll grab a bite later," he said.

"Listen, Harry," Cameron said as they moved down the hall, "I'm not a nuclear engineer, but my opinion—for what it's worth—is that this spacecraft is N-fusion drive. The fuel, I think, is hydrogen. Scooped up as it goes along. Mass conversion to energy."

Harry looked sharply at him. Theoretically, it was possible to compress two protons and two neutrons, and with extreme heat create nuclear fusion to release a great deal of energy. But in a spacecraft? "How could they get temperatures high enough for a fusion reaction?" he asked. "It takes something like one million degrees, as far as we know."

"As far as *we* know," Cameron said. "And there's another thing. I'm just guessing again, but I don't think that ship was capable of interstellar travel. It couldn't have generated enough speed."

"How fast do you think it could go?"

"Still guessing, I'd say about five hundred thousand miles an hour."

Harry glanced at him. "That's not exactly poking along the freeway, is it?"

"But for the distances we're talking about, it's nothing. Let's say it came from 'next door,'—from Alpha Centauri, four-point-three light years away. It would've been on the road for over four thousand years. And there's something else that I think clinches it, Harry."

"What?"

"There wasn't enough food in that galley to last those guys five days. Even if they were both on a diet."

Harry frowned. "Then where did the ship come from?"

"A mother ship," Cameron said. "Something bigger and much faster than we can imagine."

Harry looked at him, considering the implications. If there was less than five days' food on the spacecraft, that would mean the mother ship had to be within sixty million miles—probably a lot closer. Which meant they were probably monitoring the spacecraft closely, and knew exactly where it was.

"Harry, this thing is getting serious. We need some high-powered experts to help us. We're not just dealing with a stray flying saucer that happened to fall out of the sky, and it involves a lot more than just the security of the United States. My God, the future of the whole world might be at stake!"

Harry nodded, knowing it was true. And Sarah and Paul Bannister had made the same appeal for help thirty minutes ago. From the alien's heart tissue, they couldn't tell if the man was thirty-five years old, or a hundred and five. Nor had they figured out the cause of death yet. They wanted the other body shipped somewhere to be examined by expert pathologists.

Harry rubbed his eyes and let out a long sigh. "Morrison asked me to keep the crew small. I said we could do the job. Now what do I say?"

"We didn't even know what the job was, Harry. So say you were wrong. Say you've got a bunch of incompetents on your hands. Say anything—but tell him you need help. All the help you can get."

"Okay," Harry said wearily. "I'll call him right now." He walked off toward the conference room, dreading the call. But the more he thought about it, the more he realized Cameron was right.

The whole UFO affair had gotten completely out of hand, General Morrison told himself as his aide drove him south from the Pentagon toward the suburbs of Alexandria. It was drizzling in Washington, and he gazed vacantly out the side window, feeling trapped and frustrated. He had been a fool to let Gordon Cain talk him into keeping the spacecraft discovery a secret. And now he was caught between Forbes and Cain, with no reasonable way to extricate himself.

Normal procedure would have bucked the whole thing through military channels to the Joint Chiefs, and then on to the president, where it should have gone. Then, if the president wanted to keep it secret, fine. But now it had gone too far. And if what Harry Forbes had told him was true, it could very well involve national security.

Gordon Cain had refused to talk about it on the phone. "I'm sure the situation is not as critical as Mr. Forbes presents it, General," he had said. "I'll tell you what, I'm just about to leave the office. Why don't you drive down to my home and we can discuss the whole thing thoroughly over a drink. Let me give you my address."

The idea of a thorough discussion of the matter was fine with Morrison. But he had no intention of letting this thing go on any longer. Either Cain or the president had to make it clear to the Joint Chiefs that the decision to keep the UFO matter secret had been the sole responsibility of the White House.

And if Cain refused? Morrison did not want to

answer that question. And he was determined not to let himself get into a position where he would have to.

They were in a residential district now, the big colonial and Georgian houses set far back from the street. The driver slowed and finally turned through the opened gates in a high brick wall. From there he followed the curving driveway up to the front of a well-lighted mansion. "About an hour, I think, Sergeant," Morrison said, letting himself out of the car.

An elderly housekeeper answered the door. But as quickly as she took his hat and coat, an extraordinarily attractive woman in her late thirties came smiling toward him, hand extended. "General Morrison, I'm so delighted to meet you. I'm Beverly Cain, Gordon's wife. He's told me so many nice things about you."

"My pleasure, Mrs. Cain."

She took him by the arm and guided him along the plush carpets of a central hallway. "Gordon's in the den talking on the phone at the moment. That's about all he does when he comes home, I'm afraid."

She opened the door for him, but didn't enter. "Can I have Joanna get you something to eat, General?"

"No, I'm fine, thank you, Mrs. Cain."

"Well, please let me know if we can get you anything." She looked in and smiled at her husband, then closed the door.

Gordon Cain was sitting behind an ornate desk, swiveling gently from side to side as he listened to someone on the phone. He smiled at Morrison and pointed to a big leather chair in front of a fireplace.

"Well, the polls are saying New York is fifty-fifty," he said in the phone, "but I think the weather is going to be a big factor. If we can get rain or snow, a low turn-out can tip it for us. No . . . Right . . . And have a good trip, Mr. President."

Cain sat thoughtfully at his desk for a minute, then rose, smiling. "Scotch, bourbon, vodka? What can I get you, General?"

Morrison had resolved to decline any drinks and to keep the discussion strictly on a business level. But Cain was already dropping ice cubes into two glasses. "Bourbon with some water will be fine," he said.

"I've been thinking about what Mr. Forbes told you," Cain said as he brought the drinks over and eased into the other chair. "It seems to me he is making a number of rather shaky assumptions—along with some rather far-fetched conjectures based on those assumptions. As I understand it, this man, Cameron, admits he is not a nuclear physicist or engineer. Yet he has expressed the opinion that the spacecraft is powered by some kind of nuclear fusion."

"That's true, Mr. Cain, but . . ."

"Excuse me, General. Let me finish, if I may. Using this uneducated assumption, Cameron has surmised that the craft can travel no faster than five hundred thousand miles per hour. Therefore, Forbes and Cameron have decided that there must be a mother ship hovering somewhere near earth. And yet there have been no reports of such a craft by Norad, or NASA. Or by anyone else for that matter."

"Sixty million miles is a big radius, Mr. Cain. That could put it beyond Mars. A space ship at that distance would not be picked up by the usual scans."

"Nevertheless, General, you'll have to admit that we can hardly act on the advice of people who are making guesses in a field far beyond their knowledge."

"That's precisely the point, Mr. Cain. Forbes is asking for experts. He wants some nuclear physicists and engineers to examine the craft. And they need expert pathologists to examine the bodies of the two dead men."

"I understand, General. But you must understand that we can't have people going in and out of that hangar as if it were a department store." He shook his head. "We have to stall."

Morrison took a deep breath and leaned forward. "Mr. Cain, do you realize what's happened? What that spacecraft means? What we're sitting on in Hangar 18? An election can't possibly be more important than . . ."

"But it is," Cain interrupted.

"I don't think you understand, Mr. Cain. This . . ."

"I *do* understand, General. But what you must understand is that there are other problems. And they are a lot bigger and more complex than you realize. Let me try to explain." He rose and moved to the fireplace. He gazed silently at the mantel for a minute, then turned around. "I've been with Duncan Tyler a long time, General. Twenty years. I made him a congressman. I made him a senator. I made him president. *I* did it, not Tyler."

General Morrison really didn't want to hear any more political discussions. But Gordon Cain obviously wasn't going to listen to anything the general had to say until he gave his little speech.

Cain shrugged and smiled sardonically. "Oh, Duncan Tyler's a good man. He's everybody's idea of what a president should look like. And he can make a good speech without saying one damn thing. He has only one problem. He's stupid."

The word shocked Morrison. He had never had a particularly high regard for Duncan Tyler's intelligence. But he had never expected to hear the man's closest friend and adviser describe him as stupid.

Cain's smile had turned cold. "Who do you think has been running this country for the last four years, General?" He shook his head, letting that sink in. "And I like the job. I want to keep it for another four years. And then . . . I want a promotion."

Morrison was too stunned to speak. All the things he had heard about Gordon Cain were obviously true. What was shocking was to hear the man admit it to a relative outsider.

"I've made a lot of friends in the party," Cain went on. "I've got a lot of IOU's I can call in. So if Tyler's re-elected and then endorses me when his second term is over, I will have the party's nomination in my pocket. After that, the election will be no problem at all. Then I will officially be occupying the Oval Office."

It could happen, Morrison realized. In fact, unless something unforeseen toppled his apple cart, it probably would happen.

"General," Cain said, smiling at him now, "I've always operated on one fundamental principle of politics. An old cliche that still works . . . Reward your friends and punish your enemies. The president . . . if he's re-elected, of course, . . . is going to be looking for a new chairman of the Joint Chiefs of Staff next spring. You know, of course, that General Curry will be retiring."

Morrison felt his neck grow warm. What Cain was offering was a straight-out bribe. In politics, he knew high-level jobs were exchanged for favors every day. But offering to trade the chairmanship of the Joint Chiefs . . . it was insulting.

"Mr. Cain, I am a professional soldier. I have . . ."

"Of course you are," Cain said. "And I have the highest respect for your integrity. If I didn't, I wouldn't consider you for a moment. In fact, you would not even be in my home." He moved back to his chair and eased down. "Something you must realize, General, is that the chairman of the Joint Chiefs of Staff has to be more than a first-rank military man. He has to have the respect and trust of the president. Without that, neither man can function efficiently in his job. What I'm saying is simple. I trust you and respect you. I want you to replace General Curry next spring. If the president is re-elected, that is exactly what will happen. But obviously, we're going to have to resolve that Hangar 18 situation first."

Morrison felt numb. Being chairman of the Joint Chiefs was a dream he had reserved for ten years from now. He had to have time to think about it. But he knew there was no time.

Gordon Cain was gazing calmly at him, neither

smiling nor frowning. To him it was just another day of White House business, another negotiation.

Morrison took a sip of his drink and set it aside. "Mr. Cain . . . can I call you when I get home?"

"Certainly," Cain said and rose. "I don't want to rush you into a decision you might later regret." He walked Morrison to the door. "I'm sure everything is going to work out fine. These things usually do, no matter how complicated they seem."

Morrison nodded and pulled on his coat. "By the way," he said, "Forbes asked about the girl they found in the spacecraft. Have you heard what her condition is?"

Cain shook his head. "Very bad, as I understand it. She hasn't regained consciousness yet." He smiled and shook Morrison's hand. "It's been a pleasure, General."

In the car, the general rested his head back and closed his eyes. He had not liked Gordon Cain since their first meeting in the White House. Now he found himself despising the man. And what fueled his hatred was the knowledge that everything Cain had said tonight was probably true. Duncan Tyler *was* a stupid man. And considering the ways of politicians, the likelihood of Gordon Cain becoming president of the United States four years from now was very strong.

So what did that mean for General Frank Morrison? The damnable part of it was that if he refused to go along with Cain, it would mean there was no possibility of his *ever* becoming chairman of the Joint Chiefs. Cain would certainly see to that. Even worse, it was highly unlikely that he would even see a promotion to four-star level.

The other damnable side of it was that if Tyler lost the election, the chances of his getting his fourth star were equally slim.

At his apartment, Morrison said a brief hello to his wife, then closed the door to his den and made himself another drink. He took it to his desk, placed it squarely in the center of the desk-pad and dialed the phone.

"Forbes," he said when Harry answered at Hangar 18, "we've got to hold off for another week or so. I'm sorry, but it's just too risky to allow any more people to know about that UFO."

"Risky!? General, it's a damned sight more risky *not* letting more people in here! It could be disastrous!"

"I'm sorry, Forbes, but that's the way it has to be."

"By whose orders, General?"

Morrison felt himself stiffen. He was not accustomed to being questioned by subordinates. "The orders came directly from the White House, Mr. Forbes."

A long sigh came through the phone. "I see. All right, General. We'll hang on."

"By the way, Harry," Morrison said in a friendlier tone, "that girl still hasn't come out of the coma. I'm afraid it doesn't look good."

Harry grunted his disappointment. "Okay, I'll keep in touch."

"What you have here," Professor Mills said, lifting the rock from his desk, "are two pieces of sandstone fused together. A bit of quartz in one of them . . . some volcanic ash in the other. All quite common in the area where you found it."

Steve and Lew had checked out of their motel at ten-thirty and come directly to the campus. The news was disappointing.

"Could it have been melted like this by the heat from a spacecraft engine?" Steve asked.

Mills shrugged. "Probably. But there are several dozen other sources of heat that could generate temperatures sufficient to do the same thing. You could probably do it with a blow-torch."

"So there's no radiation? Or unknown elements in it?"

"Afraid not."

Lew squinted sourly at the rock. "So, what have we got?"

"What you have here, Mr. Price, is a rock that's been subjected to a great deal of heat." Mills smiled sympathetically. "That's all. If you want to prove the Air Force is concealing a flying saucer, you'll need more substantial evidence than this, I'm afraid. Otherwise, you're just another nut."

"How about you, Professor? Do you think we're nuts?"

"No. Not at all. As a matter of fact, I believe you. But ultimately, my opinion means nothing." He smiled and sat back, his fingertips touching in front of him. "I believe you witnessed something extraordinary. If what you're suggesting is so, you're talking about the most significant event in the history of mankind. The implications are enormous . . . almost beyond our comprehension. And . . ." he shrugged again, ". . . no one is going to believe you . . . unless you have proof."

Lew sighed and stared at the rock again. "I guess, we were counting on a little more help."

"I wish I *could* help you more. But it would be wrong for me to be anything but totally honest about the situation you're in. The United States government is a very powerful institution."

Lew snorted. "Of the people, by the people, and for the people."

Mills smiled again. "Perhaps the word *certain* should be inserted before the word *people* in each case."

"Professor," Steve said, "if you were one of the 'certain' people, where would you hide a flying saucer?"

"A military base," Lew said before Mills could answer. "It's the only place they could have any guarantee of security."

Mills nodded agreement. "And if the Air Force found it, I'm inclined to think they would take it to an

Air Force base, rather than tell the army about it. However, I think there might be another requirement. Something not so easy to find."

"What?" Steve asked.

"A flying saucer is a totally unknown commodity. Who knows how far it came from, or what kind of creatures were piloting it? There might be the danger of disease, or radiation, chemical poisons, . . . any number of things that could be extremely hazardous to humans." He smiled. "Again we have the paranoia. However, in this case the paranoia would be justifiable. The Air Force, of course, would be quite aware of these dangers. They would want to protect themselves. They would also want to take it some place that has the facilities that would enable them to study the craft and its occupants."

"The lunar receiving station," Lew said.

Mills nodded. "Certainly a possibility. Or some place like it."

"There isn't anything like it," Lew said. "It's got all the instruments, the lead-lined walls, radiation detectors, . . . everything. Hangar 18!"

"There are four other air bases closer to where the thing landed," Steve countered. "Besides, Hangar 18 is a NASA facility. It isn't an Air Force base anymore."

"What are those?" Lew snorted. "The rules? The Air Force is going to step on whoever they have to in this. Like we're taking the flak for Gates' death. Right?!"

Steve gnawed the inside of his mouth for a minute, then looked at Mills. "What do you think, Professor?"

Mills shrugged. "If the Air Force people have any brains at all, they certainly would have considered Hangar 18. And unless they have a secret facility somewhere else that can do the same thing, the choices are limited."

"Steve," Lew said passionately, "we hustled our

117

butts off to get into the NASA program. Everything we've worked for is on the line here. And not only for us, maybe for a lot of other people, too. I don't think we should sit back and wait for the roof to fall in. We've got to go for something."

"Yeah," Steve finally said. "All right. Let's go."

At 3:22 P.M., Washington, D.C., time, the gray phone at the side of Lafferty's desk buzzed softly. He let it ring a second time, then lifted the receiver to his ear. "Yes?"

"Wilson. They filed a flight plan for Midland, Texas."

"Midland?"

"That's fifty miles from Hangar 18."

Lafferty settled back in his chair. "How did the geology report come out?"

"No problem. It was negative. Just a rock."

Lafferty smiled faintly at the irony. He had lost two men trying to get that rock back. "How did they find out about Hangar 18?"

"I got no idea."

It was simple, Lafferty decided; they were smart. And that could lead to trouble. "Okay," he said, "you'd better stop them. Permanently this time. Make it look like an accident."

"Will do," the voice said and clicked off.

Lafferty pulled another phone over and dialed the White House. "Lafferty," he said when Gordon Cain came on. "You going to be near a phone for the rest of the day, Mr. Cain?"

"Why? What's the problem?"

"No problem. I expect the matter to be resolved this afternoon or tonight. But if any important decisions have to be made, I like to know you're available."

"I'll be home tonight."

"Fine," Lafferty said and hung up.

XI

Steve Bancroft still felt uneasy about flying to Midland, Texas, and driving another fifty miles to Hangar 18. He could imagine finding an abandoned Air Force base and nothing but dust and cobwebs in the hangar. Which would leave them out in the boondocks, fifty miles from anywhere.

From the Tucson airport he had called Flo Matson at NASA again, but she still hadn't received any straight answers from the Air Force. General Heller in Washington had told her that he had seen no official documents charging anyone with negligence in Gates' death. But he refused to make any public statements to that effect. Instead, he was instituting an inquiry to determine the source of the newspaper story. When the inquiry was completed—in three or four weeks, he guessed—he would then be in a position to comment.

In the meantime, a hundred other newspapers across the country had printed abbreviated accounts of the newspaper story. They avoided slander by not reprinting the story itself, and the reports were full of phrases like: "The *Bulletin* story alleged" and "according to the unconfirmed story in the. . . ." Either way, it all added up to the same thing. The public was being told that Steve Bancroft and Lew Price had done something highly questionable on that shuttle flight.

As to the UFO, Flo had received nothing more than a dozen or so "no comments," and a considerable amount of laughter when she tried to trace it through the Air Force. "There's not much you can do but hang in there," she finally told Steve. "Either that saucer'll show up somewhere, or in six or eight weeks time the Air Force will complete its 'three week' inquiry."

At the Midland airport they rented a car, and were told it would be ready in fifteen minutes. Forty-five minutes later, and after four cups of coffee, the rental booth girl found them in the coffee shop, apologized for the fourth time and handed over the car keys.

"You know what that Air Force inquiry report will say," Lew said when they finally got the car out of the parking lot. " 'Although technically the pilot and the shuttle commander did not deviate substantially from standard procedures, questions might be raised concerning their behavior in what might be considered unusual circumstances, to wit, the necessity while in flight of the accompanying Air Force officer to exit the vehicle and initiate repairs on an item—a secret item—being transported in the cargo hold of said space vehicle.' "

Steve laughed and swung the car onto the highway. "You should get a job writing Air Force manuals."

"Yeah. It's great language. You cover all bases, say nothing, and make sure nobody understands it. Then you form a committee to study the report." Lew shook his head. "You know, I'm getting sick of the whole damned thing. What was it that guy said in that *Network* movie? 'I'm mad as hell, and I'm not going to take it anymore!' "

"Well, . . . NASA's not that bad."

"No, it isn't. But it's getting squashed by the Air Force. We're not astronauts anymore. We're not going to the moon, or Mars, or Jupiter. We're truck drivers. Every piddling dime we get is spent to take some kind of Air Force peeping tom up into orbit. 'Take this up to six hundred miles and blast it into orbit. But don't peek at it. And don't ask any questions. You ask questions, fella, and we'll have the FBI checking out your garbage can. Just keep your eyes shut, and your nose clean, and drive that shuttle where we tell you to.' It stinks, Steve. Your friend Mills was right. This whole country is becoming the United States of Paranoia."

Steve laughed. "And then there's the Union of Soviet Socialistic Paranoiacs."

"Right. And the Paranoiac People's Republic of China." Lew grinned and squinted at the road ahead. A temporary sign said *Slow—Construction Ahead,* and yellow lights were blinking on the crest of a hill. He glanced at his watch. "We're just about going to make it before dark." The sun was beginning to set behind them, turning the eastern sky a pale pink.

"Unless the road is out," Steve commented.

From the top of the hill they could see a mile-long stretch of highway, all scattered with trenches, flashing lights and temporary barriers. Apparently the workmen had knocked off for the day.

"Hey," Lew said as they started down the hill, "you oughta slow down a little."

Steve had already hit the brakes once. The pedal had gone down to within an inch of the floor before anything happened. He hit it again, this time jamming the pedal down hard.

Nothing! This time there was no resistance at all; his foot dropped freely to the floor. "Lew!" he said, pumping again. "The brakes . . . they're gone!"

The speedometer was climbing past forty-five now. They were flying past barriers, weaving from one side of the highway to the other to avoid the trenches.

"The emergency brake!" Lew shouted. "Hit it!"

Steve jammed his left foot on the emergency pedal. It hit bottom with no resistance. "Nothing!"

The speedometer needle was approaching sixty, but it seemed like they were going twice that fast. On the left side of the highway there was now nothing but barriers and a deep trench. On the right, the shoulder dropped off at least eight feet. There was nowhere to go but straight ahead. And the downhill slope was growing steeper through the next mile.

"Steve!" Lew shouted. He pointed at a narrow asphalt road curving off to the right about a quarter of a mile ahead.

Steve nodded, gripping the wheel tightly. The curve was gradual enough that he thought he could make it. After that the road was almost level, curving broadly around a low hill. He tried the brakes. Once again there was nothing.

The tires began to howl and the car leaned heavily as he edged to the side and swung gradually into the curve. Silently, they both prayed that no cars would appear coming in the other direction. The wheels were chattering, throwing gravel off the edge, and Steve was barely able to hold the car from going off the left side.

Once around the hill, the road straightened. But the sight before them was no more comforting. The road went straight down the hill to a gate in a chain link fence. Behind the fence were what looked like twenty or thirty acres of huge tanks and pipes and cracking towers, all painted silver and white. *West Texas Consolidated Refinery*, a sign on one of the storage tanks said.

There was no place else to go. On either side of the road the drop-off was still at least ten feet. And by the time it flattened out they would be too close to the fence to make a turn.

Steve hit the horn ring and held it down. Inside the gate a man in a suntan uniform gaped at them for an instant, then ran at full speed to the side.

"Hang on!" Steve said and took a sharp breath. Lew instinctively turned to the side and ducked his head.

They tore through with one wrenching screech. Wire and pipe from the fence went flying in all directions. The car swiveled dangerously to the side, its speed diminished by no more than half. Steve straightened it, and then they were whipping past steel buildings and a tangled jungle of pipes. He pumped the brake pedal again, but still nothing happened. Two hundred yards ahead of them the road ended at the solid white wall of what looked like a million-gallon storage tank.

"The fence!" Lew shouted.

Steve responded immediately. On the left was a six-foot chain link fence running all the way to the tank. He swung the car into it at a shallow angle, and once again they both ducked. Three long seconds later, the car wrenched to a stop, the front end resting against a tangle of wire and bent posts. They were less than twenty feet from the steel tank.

Steve finally let out his breath. "You okay?" he asked shakily.

Lew nodded and slowly unbuckled his safety belt. "I think so." He pushed the door open and stepped out, surveying the wreckage. The car didn't look too bad. But a couple of hundred feet of fencing was in shambles behind them. Steve came around the other side of the car, stepping gingerly over the tangled wire. There didn't seem to be much doubt about what had happened to the brakes. Somebody in Midland must have flashed a badge at the rental car people. Then they had borrowed the car for awhile and probably loosened a couple of the hydraulic bleed valves. Just enough so the brakes would last until they got to the highway and picked up some speed.

"Lew!" Steve suddenly said.

He was staring at the front gate of the refinery. A black sedan was coming through, maneuvering cautiously over the rubble inside the gate. The two men in the front seat were wearing dark suits and neckties, both of them bent forward, peering sharply through the windshield.

"What do you think?"

There was no need for an answer. Once past the rubble, the car roared forward, and a hand with a pistol came out of the window on the passenger side. The gun fired almost instantaneously. The bullet slammed through the rear window of the rental car.

They both ducked and ran. Behind the mangled fence was an endless jungle of pipes and pumps and tanks with narrow walkways between them. They ran the distance of a city block, then changed direction toward the back of the refinery. Behind them, they heard the car screech to a stop and then the slam of two doors.

Other than the two gunmen and the uniformed man they had seen at the gate, the place didn't seem to have another soul in it. "We passed a big tanker truck near the front gate," Lew said when they paused for breath. "If we could work our way back there, maybe the keys are in it."

Steve nodded, and they moved on. They circled broadly back toward the front gate, seeing no sign of the two men. Five minutes later, they paused again, staying well hidden within a niche of pipes. They were back to within a hundred feet of the road now.

"Listen, Lew," Steve said between breaths. "This is all crazy, and I can't figure what's going on. But one of us has got to get to that hangar, or get in touch with Harry Forbes somehow. Harry's being on a top secret assignment might have something to do with the saucer. But I know damned well he wouldn't get mixed up in this sort of thing. These guys are professional killers."

"But why?"

Steve shook his head. "It's got to be the Air Force. That phony story on us was the first step. It was supposed to wipe out our credibility. If we talk about a flying saucer, it looks like we're trying to cover up our negligence by claiming the saucer caused Gates' death. So we look like idiots. And the Air Force hoped we'd just pull into our shells and keep our mouths shut. When we didn't, they got scared. And the closer we get to Hangar 18, the more panicked they're getting. You were right, Lew. The saucer's got to be there. And I'll bet Harry, and Phil Cameron, are there too. I'll bet they're locked up in there with no communication with the outside except through the Air Force."

"Harry wouldn't go for that," Lew said.

"He would if he doesn't know he's a prisoner—if they've convinced him they've got to keep the place secure against leaks. Harry wouldn't think twice about it. If he's locked up with a flying saucer, the only thing he'd be interested in is that saucer."

Lew nodded. "Yeah. I think you're right. Let's get to the truck."

They were in luck for a change. The tanker was a brand new rig, and the keys were dangling from the ignition switch. It was standing about a hundred yards from the gate, facing in the right direction. They reached it from the side, coming through a bed of horizontal pipes, and neither of the two gunmen were anywhere in sight. Steve took the driver's side, and they climbed quietly into the cab, neither of them closing his door just yet.

"You know how to drive this thing?" Lew asked.

"I'm going to learn awfully fast."

There was a clutch, and two gear-shift levers, each with a chart showing the shift patterns. Steve put both of them in the "2" position, pushed in the clutch, and turned the key. He would probably burn the clutch plates a little. But he didn't want to start out at a crawl. The engine kicked over and rumbled smoothly. "Okay, let's go," he said, and they both slammed their doors.

"Hey!" someone shouted behind them. In the big rearview mirror, Steve saw a man running toward them from one of the buildings. He gunned the motor and let out the clutch.

"Steve! Look out!"

He saw them as quickly as the truck started moving. The two men in dark suits were running toward them from the gate. They both stopped suddenly, their guns lifted. Steve jammed the throttle to the floor and

125

ducked as the first two bullets tore through the windshield and slammed into the back of the cab.

When he lifted his head again, the men were gone. The truck was rolling over the rubble and going out the gate. He shifted the gears, then shifted again, trying to get the right ones. They were picking up speed, but not very fast.

"This thing is loaded with gas."

"You're doing fine," Lew said, watching the mirror on his side. "But I think we're going to have company again."

When they reached the highway and started down the long slope, the black sedan was coming up close behind them. The sound of a pistol shot came faintly from the rear. Then a second and a third.

Lew grimaced. "You know if this truck takes a bullet, it's not gonna help the gas shortage any."

"Or *us,* pal," Steve added.

Lew opened the glove compartment. He rummaged through it for a minute, then pulled out a highway flare. He immediately opened the cab door and started out.

"What're you doing?" Steve yelled.

"Trust me," Lew shouted back, and disappeared.

"Lew! Get back in here! Lew!!"

Lew reappeared suddenly, this time in the mirror on the right side of the cab. He was working his way along a narrow ledge that ran toward the back of the truck. What the hell was he up to?! Behind them, the men were still firing, a shot coming every four or five seconds. It sounded like they were aiming carefully now.

Were they trying for the tires? Or trying to hit Lew? Steve edged the truck to the right side, almost into the shoulder, hoping to cut off their firing angle on Lew. Then he caught his breath, glancing quickly back and forth from the windshield to the side mirror.

Was he hit? Or had he just slipped? One of Lew's legs was dangling freely, the other foot groping to get a hold on the railing. He finally got both feet up, and he was moving toward the back again. Then he stretched out and reached for something below him.

Steve looked at the left-side mirror. Behind them, the black car was swerving off to the right and then back again. Apparently the driver was trying to give the other man a better shot at Lew. Steve cursed softly and edged the truck farther to the right. Then he glanced at the right mirror.

Something was trailing out behind the truck, the end of it bouncing wildly on the pavement. It was a big hose. Steve looked again and then frowned. "Oh, my God," he breathed. Gasoline was now pouring from the nozzle at the end of the hose. It was splashing wildly in all directions as the nozzle skipped and bounced crazily on the pavement.

The car had dropped back another fifty feet but it was still getting splattered with gasoline. The passenger was firing more rapidly now, as if determined to hit something before the entire car was drenched. Steve held his breath. Then he glanced at the right-hand mirror again and froze.

Lew was crouched on the ledge, hanging on to the railing with one hand. In the other hand he was holding a sputtering flare. He cocked his arm back and threw it high in the air behind the truck.

It was clear now what he was attempting to do. But Steve couldn't believe it would work. As quick as the flare left Lew's hand, Steve looked at the left mirror. Then he caught his breath as a giant fireball erupted 200 feet behind the truck. For a moment the car continued moving along the highway through the massive flames. Then it swerved off to the right, and flew down the embankment. A moment later, a roaring explosion from the car's gas tank sent burning pieces of debris rocketing off in all directions.

In the mirror, Steve could see that Lew was still clinging to the railing. But there was something strange about his position. His head was down and his right hand seemed to be grasping at his chest. Then Steve saw it: the splotch of shiny blood on the front of Lew's shirt. "Lew!" he cried out. As quickly as he shouted, Lew tumbled off the truck and disappeared from sight.

Steve hit the brakes. He jammed the pedal down as hard as he could, at the same time gripping the steering wheel. The wheels bucked for a moment. Then they locked in place, the tires screeching in protest as the rear end swung to the left and seemed to be pushing the cab off the road to the right. Steve fought the wheel, trying to swing it to the left, at the same time releasing the brakes. The truck jerked violently. Then it was crashing headlong down the embankment and into a ravine. Two seconds later, it came to a jolting stop, the nose buried in a vertical wall of dirt.

Instinctively, Steve pushed the door open and tumbled out. He landed heavily in the dirt, pulled himself up and staggered another twenty feet before he stumbled to the ground again.

He stayed on his hands and knees for a minute, breathing deeply, trying to collect himself. His head felt like a cracked watermelon. Blood was trickling from his forehead and down the edge of his nose. He finally touched the wound, realizing that his head must have hit the steering wheel when the truck came to a stop. Nausea was ballooning in his stomach. He breathed deeply, methodically fighting it back. Then he pulled himself to his feet and started climbing the embankment.

Two cars had stopped on the road above. "Are you okay?" a man asked. Steve ignored him. He started walking back to where Lew had fallen off the truck. He stumbled and caught himself. Then he picked up his pace until he was running.

Three cars had already stopped, and more were pulling over. Several of the people had gone down the embankment and were watching from a distance as the black sedan continued to burn. Next to Lew, a middle-aged man and a young girl were kneeling on the shoulder of the road. "Don't touch him," the man said to Steve. "Some people went to call an ambulance."

Lew was on his back, blinking vacantly at the sky, grimacing as waves of pain seemed to seep through his body. Steve knelt beside him and lifted his head. "Lew!"

His eyes went in and out of focus. "Steve . . ." he said in a hoarse whisper. "You're gonna be okay. An ambulance is coming."

"Find . . ." Lew took a breath and grimaced again. "Find that thing. Steve . . . don't let them get away with it."

"Lew!"

The eyes were suddenly dull. He was no longer breathing. Steve clenched his jaw tight, fighting back the sobs that were rising in his throat.

"Say, mister," the man standing next to him said, "you're hurt, too. You better lie down."

Steve lowered Lew's head gently back to the ground and looked around. More people were coming, asking what had happened, if anybody was hurt. Steve rose and strode past them. A blue Ford was parked on the shoulder of the road, empty, the motor running. He slid behind the wheel, dropped it into gear and pushed the throttle to the floor.

XII

Harry Forbes closed the looseleaf notebook in which he had been making notes for his report, and tossed it on his desk. He tossed his pen down next to it and rubbed his eyes. So far, his notes didn't add up to much. He had tried to be organized, and enter everything they learned under category headings. But the only section that filled more than a page was the one with physical descriptions and dimensions. Under *Power sources,* the notes were nothing more than Phil Cameron's guesses about N-fusion drive. Under *Communication Systems*, no definite determinations. *Weapons:* Laser-type ray. Apparently very powerful. Unable to determine range or potency without testing. *Language—Written:* Similar to Sumerian cuneiform in appearance. Also similar to inscriptions in ancient Mexican pyramid. Symbol for earth tentatively determined. *Alien Beings:* In appearance, almost identical to human beings. No equipment available for brain scans or sophisticated analysis. And on and on in a dozen more categories.

Harry felt exhausted and depressed. After the call from Morrison last night, he had tossed and turned until four o'clock in the morning, arguing with himself, trying to find some justification for the White House keeping such a tight lid on the project. He had not been very successful. He had been even less successful explaining Morrison's refusal to the others.

Paul Bannister had grudgingly accepted it. Sarah

130

Michaels had protested, saying it was the most ridiculous thing she had ever heard of. If one of the alien bodies could be shipped to New York, or even to Dallas, a dozen specialists could be working on it at the same time. With their equipment and expert lab people, they could learn more in ten minutes than she and Paul could find out in another week.

Phil Cameron was furious. "For God's sake, Harry, did you tell them what the presence of this spacecraft could mean? That there could be a hundred more of them waiting out in space somewhere? That they've got a whole library full of books and films about earth?"

"I told him," Harry had said. He hadn't been quite that specific with Morrison. But he had certainly outlined the dangerous possibilities. Then Cameron had asked a question Harry had been afraid to ask himself in the past twenty-four hours.

"Did Morrison talk directly to the president?"

"I don't know," Harry said. "I presume he did. If he didn't, I'm sure the information was passed on."

"How do you know?"

He didn't know. But it was certainly the sort of thing a man could reasonably assume. "For God's sake, Phil. Every time you gave me significant information in Houston did you question whether I passed it on to the director?"

"No, I didn't. But you're a sensible man, Harry, with no axes to grind. You're not General Morrison. And you're not in the Air Force."

"Which means you should question him even less. He's a military man. He's trained to follow the book, and do as he's told."

"You mean like General Douglas MacArthur?"

"Oh, come on, Phil. You're being paranoiac. Are you trying to say General Morrison is involved in some kind of conspiracy, or something? What possible motive could he have for keeping all this secret from the president or the Joint Chiefs?"

Cameron had finally backed off a little. "All I'm saying is that somebody, somewhere, has made a stupid decision. Whether it's the president, or the Joint Chiefs, or Morrison, not letting our best scientists and engineers—*and* doctors—look this thing over as fast as possible, is asinine. It's short-sighted and stupid. And it might be suicidal."

"Okay, Phil, I agree with you. But the decision has been made, and we have to live with it. Okay?"

"For how long?"

"About a week or so."

Cameron had snorted and walked out of the conference room. An hour later he had come to Harry's office and apologized for blowing, and they had ended up commiserating with each other. Then Cameron had laughed and quoted John Milton. "I guess we shouldn't forget, Harry, 'They also serve who only stand and wait.'"

But Harry hadn't slept very well. Nor had they made much progress during the day. In one of the lower chambers, the technicians had found an access hatch into the "platform" area of the ship. But the installations there hadn't told them much. If anything, they tended to verify Phil Cameron's theory about N-fusion power.

As far as the controls were concerned, a great many of them seemed to be functional only when the ship was in flight. So until they could break the ship down completely and analyze every minute part, they could not determine what many of the controls did. Even with the best experts in the world, that would probably take months.

Harry glanced at his watch and pulled himself out of the chair. He was getting cabin fever, he decided. He left the office and walked down the long hallway to the door leading to the outside of the hangar. How long had it been since he had seen daylight? Or even any stars? He couldn't remember. He pushed open the door and moved past the two Air Force guards, out to the center of the concrete apron. The sun was down, but only a few stars had begun to appear. Harry breathed deeply, wondering if somewhere up in that dark void a giant spaceship was sailing around between Mars and Jupiter, its commander wondering where reconnaisance craft Z-7 was? Or spaceship glom-ogel. Neal Kelso hadn't mentioned anything about numbers yet.

"Everything all right, Mr. Forbes?"

Harry turned, startled. An Air Force MP with a gold bar on his collar was standing behind him. "Everything's fine, Lieutenant. Just checking to see if the world was still out here."

"It's a nice evening, sir."

"Yes, it is." The lieutenant seemed ill at ease for some reason. Harry wondered if he knew what was inside the hangar he was guarding. Or had he simply been dropped off with his platoon, or regiment, or whatever, and been told to guard the place. "Where you from, Lieutenant?"

"Saginaw, Michigan, sir."

"How do you like Texas?"

The question apparently stumped the man, as if the ability to make personal judgments had been left behind the day he swore to protect his country from all enemies.

"I've only been here three days, sir," he finally said.

He still hadn't made a judgment; he had merely stated a fact. Harry smiled to himself, realizing he was being hyperanalytic. The lieutenant was only about twenty-five years old—probably a kid who had joined the ROTC in college to help pay for his tuition. So he was serving out his required number of years. Then he would leave the service and become an accountant, or a policeman, or maybe an advertising executive. He would get married and have a family, and be the same as every other American trying to pay his taxes and save enough money to send his kids to college.

"Yeah," he would someday say over a couple of beers, "I remember when I was with the Air Force MP's down in Texas. They had us guarding this hangar where a bunch of scientists and NASA people were holed up. I don't know what the hell they had in there, but one day a big hole was blasted right through the side of the building. Like a ray-gun, or something. A three-foot hole right through a goddamned steel wall. Honest to God."

Harry suddenly had a feeling of compassion for the boy. He hoped to God he did have a family some day. And that he could talk about a ray-gun as if it were the strangest thing on earth. He smiled and moved back toward the hangar. "Well, I'd better get back to work. Good night, Lieutenant."

"Have a nice evening, sir."

Harry felt better after his fresh air break. He strode down the hall bound for the air lock door and the hangar.

"Harry!" Paul Bannister called out from the hospital.

Harry turned back and pushed through the doors. Bannister was at the sink washing his hands. "We were just going to go looking for you."

Harry smiled. "You need another body to cut up?"

Sarah was piling instruments in the sterilizer. "No," she said, "but we found out how the aliens died."

"They were asphyxiated," Bannister said.

"Asphyxiated? How?"

"Those broken glass vials you found in the specimen room? They contained chemicals. Elements similar to potassium cyanide, a form of sulfuric acid, and several other compounds. When combined, some of them form a gas. A very toxic gas."

"It must have spread throughout the ship," Sarah added.

"But when we went in," Harry said, "our meters didn't register any dangerous substances."

Bannister shrugged. "By then it had probably been dissipated by the air conditioning. But we found traces of it in their bodies. In their lungs and blood. Some of the organs."

"Apparently the vials were jarred loose and broken," Sarah said. "Probably when the satellite hit the spacecraft."

Harry was surprised. He had assumed that people who built spaceships that traveled across galaxies were too smart to leave vials of deadly chemicals lying around. "Sort of ironic, isn't it?" he said. "They're light years ahead of us in intelligence, but they were killed by a stupid mistake."

Sarah snorted softly. "Considering that ray gun they had, maybe it's just as well."

Harry moved for the door and Bannister followed him into the hall. "Harry, did Morrison tell you anything about that girl we found on the ship?"

"Still in a coma. I guess it doesn't look good."

"Too bad. Where'd they take her?"

"I don't know. I didn't think to ask."

Bannister nodded. "I imagine they've identified her by now. It would be interesting to find out where the spacecraft picked her up."

"Yes, it would."

Harry left Bannister at the hospital doors and continued down the hallway thinking about the dead aliens. They must have died within seconds after the satellite hit them. Otherwise, the craft probably wouldn't have headed for the earth so quickly. Some kind of automatic control must have taken over immediately. Some sensor, perhaps, that detected a malfunctioning in the aliens' bodies, and switched the controls into an automatic landing pattern on the nearest planet with a safe environment? An interesting thought—and not too unreasonable.

Neal Kelso was in the computer room, sipping

coffee and staring at printed read-outs as they came rattling out of the machine. The floor around him was littered ankle-deep in discarded sheets.

Harry paused at the door. "How's it coming, Neal?"

Kelso turned and stared at him as if unsure who he was. His eyes were red and he had a two-day stubble of whiskers. "Huh? Oh. It's coming, Harry. I'm getting it. About one word in ten."

"What are the tenth words?"

Kelso shook his head. "They don't make much sense so far. There's one symbol that reappears fairly often. I think it refers to some kind of animal. Maybe a domestic animal, like a dog or cat. I've even figured out the distinction between the symbols for the male and female of the animal. Other than that . . ."

Kelso turned back to the computer, and Harry moved on. That's all they needed—the discovery that the aliens were dog and cat lovers, and all the books in their library were about Lassie and Felix the Cat. Considering the pictures they had of earth, however, that didn't seem likely.

On the flight deck of the spacecraft, Phil Cameron was eased back in one of the couches, staring at pictures on the big viewing screen. "Look at this stuff, Harry," he said as Harry came up the elevator.

"What is it?"

"I don't know."

Harry moved to the other couch and sat down. On the screen some kind of map of the universe came into focus. Then it dissolved into pictures of planets in our solar system, each of them identified with a symbol. Each picture also had a grid pattern over it, and as a picture would draw closer to a planet, the small cuneiform characters on the coordinates of the grid pattern constantly changed.

"They must be navigational aids," Harry said.

"That's what I figured. Now look at what's coming up."

The next picture showed the earth, along with the symbol they had already identified. But this time, the earth symbol had some additional cuneiform characters next to it, and a grid pattern overlaid the picture.

The picture dissolved, and closer and closer shots of the earth came into focus. Then, suddenly, there were close shots of missile silos, nuclear power plants, various industrial complexes. Then shots of a dozen or more large cities: New York, London, Paris, Moscow . . . each of them with a grid pattern and two sets of characters at the bottom of the picture. Finally the pictures faded away.

Harry frowned and shook his head. "All those are things I suppose they would be interested in. How we live, how far we've advanced technologically . . ."

"But why the grid patterns and the notations on each of them?"

Harry shrugged. "Hard to say. Neal's making some progress with his translations. If he has a little more luck, maybe he'll be able to figure them out."

Cameron nodded and pushed some buttons. Soft music suddenly came through the speakers.

Harry looked at him. "Where's that coming from?"

"It's a local radio station," Cameron said. "Probably Lubbock or Abilene. Maybe Dallas. I finally figured out how our friends monitored those radio and TV broadcasts."

Harry nodded. It was pleasant to hear something from the outside world again. He told Cameron how the aliens died, and his theory about the ship switching to an automatic landing pattern.

Cameron sat back and thought about it. "Makes sense," he said. Then he frowned and gave Harry a narrow look. "Harry . . . if they had an automatic landing system, wouldn't it also follow that they would have some kind of an alarm transmitter? Like a radio-beeper sending out the position of the crashed spacecraft? Even our little private planes have those."

Harry nodded thoughtfully. That had not occurred to him. But it was reasonable. If they cared enough about their men, or the craft, to put in the automatic landing system, they must be interested in recovering the spacecraft. Which probably meant that somewhere on this ship a signal was being transmitted right now.

"Harry," Cameron said quietly, "I think we might consider another possibility. With all their sophisticated monitoring equipment, I think it's very possible, . . . maybe probable . . . that they have something even better than a radio-beeper signal."

Harry looked sharply at him. "Like what?"

"I think it's very possible they are monitoring everything we're doing here. That there are microphones, and TV cameras, and maybe other kinds of scanning devices watching us right now."

Harry stared at him, then glanced around the cockpit, feeling his heartbeat increase a notch. The idea was not too far-fetched. "The TV camera . . . the one that scans the exterior . . ."

Cameron nodded. "The signal could be transmitted to the mother ship at the same time the picture is displayed in here."

"Good God," Harry breathed. "And they could be listening to us right now . . ."

"It's possible."

Harry suddenly felt exposed and very vulnerable. His thoughts raced back over the last couple of days, considering the things they had said or done in the spacecraft. How would those things be interpreted by somebody listening, or watching? He could think of nothing that would particularly anger anybody—assuming the aliens were capable of anger, or any of the other human emotions. Mostly what they would have learned was that Harry Forbes and his crew of scientists were relatively ignorant and incompetent. But he was glad that he had mentioned how the aliens had died. At least Harry and his staff could not be suspected of murder.

Cameron laughed uneasily, and glanced around the cabin. "It's eerie."

Harry nodded. "And maybe not true," he said. He pulled himself up from the couch. "And if we're going to get any work done, I think we're better off to assume it is not true."

"Yeah," Cameron said uncertainly.

Harry moved to the elevator, then stopped as the music on the speakers suddenly went silent and an announcer's voice broke in.

"We interrupt our regular programming to bring you a news bulletin," the man said. "Lewis Price, a NASA space shuttle pilot, has been killed in a local traffic accident this afternoon. An injured man who reportedly left the scene of the accident has been identified as Steven Bancroft, a NASA space shuttle commander. Bancroft and Price have been the target of charges that they were responsible for the death of an Air Force officer during a recent shuttle flight. More details as they become available."

Harry and Paul Cameron stared incredulously at each other as the soft music came back on. "Jesus . . ." Cameron breathed. "A traffic accident? Lew . . .? What do they mean, charges . . . ?"

Harry's heart felt like it had dropped through the floor. Lew Price dead?! He couldn't believe it. A local traffic accident? "Where is that broadcast coming from?"

Cameron shook his head. "I don't know. There's no dial to find the kilocycles."

Harry turned quickly back to the elevator and Cameron scrambled after him.

"Harry, I just heard about it myself," General Morrison said almost as quickly as he picked up the phone. "I don't know anything more about it than you do. It was a traffic accident in Texas somewhere, as I understand it."

"And what about the charges that Lew and Steve were responsible for Gates' death?! You must have known about that, General!"

"Yes, . . . yes, I heard about them."

"Why didn't you tell me?!"

"I've been looking into it, Harry . . . trying to find out where the story came from. There's an official inquiry . . ."

Morrison was stumbling and stammering enough that Harry knew he was lying. "General, I want to see Bancroft. And I want to know if Lew's death had anything to do with what they saw up there in space. I want to know if it has anything to do with what we have here in Hangar 18!"

"There's no connection, Harry, I can assure you."

"That's not good enough," Harry said flatly. "I want to talk to Bancroft myself! And if he isn't here by morning, I'm going to walk out of this place and make a statement to the press. And you won't like what I'm going to say, General. NASA's not taking the rap for this."

Morrison's voice turned cold. "You don't understand, Harry. It's more complicated than that."

"I understand a great deal, General. And you'd better understand that if anything happens to Steve Bancroft, I'm holding you personally responsible!" Harry banged the phone down, and dropped back in his chair.

"You think he'll produce Steve?" Cameron asked.

"He'd better."

XIII

In the semi-darkness of his Pentagon office, General Morrison quietly replaced the phone in its cradle and gazed emptily across the room.

Somehow he had known that call would be coming from Harry Forbes. Forty-five minutes ago he had left his office, intending to take the elevator down to the first floor and have his aide drive him directly to General Curry's dinner party. But then a casual remark by the chief petty officer logging him out of the restricted area had stopped him cold.

The man had asked if the general had heard about the astronaut being killed down in Texas. At first Morrison thought he was referring to Colonel Gates. But then the man went on. "Three people were killed from what I heard, sir. The other two got burned to death."

"Do you know the astronaut's name?" Morrison had asked.

"It was Lew Price, sir. The same man that was in the shuttle when Colonel Gates got killed."

Morrison's heart had sunk. He had already signed himself out of the log book. He mumbled some excuse to the petty officer, signed himself in again and walked numbly back to his office.

He could get very little information about the accident in Texas. It had happened somewhere east of Midland. A gasoline truck was involved somehow, and two men in a black car had been burned beyond recognition. Steve Bancroft had also been there, it seemed, and he had stolen a car and driven away.

The only thing that General Morrison was reasonably certain about was that Gordon Cain was in some way responsible for that accident. And it also seemed highly probable that Lew Price and Steve Bancroft were trying to get to Hangar 18. There was no other reason for them to be in that area. The only remaining question was: How quickly would Harry Forbes hear about it?

Morrison knew it wouldn't take long. People listened to radios—even technicians working with computers in old Air Force hangars.

And then the call had come from Forbes.

So where did it end? he wondered now. It seemed like years ago that he was at Mission Control in Houston, giving the order to continue the countdown on that satellite launch. A different decision then, and he would be at General Curry's house right now.

Or a different decision in Houston when he called Gordon Cain instead of reporting first to the Pentagon. It had all seemed so urgent then. A saucer was coming down, and Norad was tracking it. They knew exactly where it was going to land. The president should know first.

But Gordon Cain had never told the president.

At his house last night, Cain had admitted it. That's when Morrison should have insisted that the whole thing be turned over to the Joint Chiefs and the president. Instead, he had let Cain's flattery and promises lure him more deeply into the whole mess.

And now it was too late. Harry Forbes knew exactly what was going on. One of his shuttle men was dead. And whether the other one was delivered to the hangar or not, Forbes was going to tell the whole story.

And then tomorrow, or at least by the next day, Morrison would be summoned to General Curry's office. Or maybe it would be done more formally than that; a written order advising him that he was immediately relieved of all duties, and that he must report to the Adjutant General's office no later than. . . .

He felt sick. His throat was dry and his heart was thumping with slow, sledgehammer blows against his breastbone. But he had to make the call; he had to tell Cain about Forbes.

He took a long breath and dialed.

Cain listened in silence. Morrison told him everything that Forbes had said. And then he felt his voice turn hoarse as he added, "And all we needed was two weeks."

"You did everything you could, General," Cain said quietly. "The Bancroft and Price situation just got out of hand."

"Someone killed him," Morrison said.

"Yes, I know," Cain answered, his voice even softer. "Go home, General. Don't worry about it."

"What happened, Mr. Cain? How was it done? Who did it?"

"That's not important, General. Just go home, have a few drinks and relax. Think about your future."

"My future?! Do you realize what's . . ."

"Go home, General! Forget about it. I'll call you tomorrow."

"Cain . . . !" Morrison shouted, but the phone was dead.

Wolf Air Force Base was obviously occupied. From the road a quarter of a mile away, Steve Bancroft could see lights in the small office by the front gate. And the man inside was wearing an Air Force uniform. A half mile beyond the gate and the rows of barracks, the hangar area off to the right was also lighted with floodlights. That's where Hangar 18 had to be.

Steve had pulled off to the side of the road twenty minutes earlier. His head was pounding, and several times while he had been driving eastward, nausea had welled into his throat and he had come close to passing out. And the occasional double-vision told him fairly clearly that he was suffering from a concussion. But he had to get inside that hangar. Harry Forbes had to be in there.

A few miles back he had stopped at a gas station and tried to call the air base. But no such number was listed. "That place closed up years ago, honey," the operator told him.

"But I understood they installed some phones just recently," Steve tried. "Within the past four or five days."

"Not through this office," she said. "Least they never told me about it."

It was about what he expected. General Morrison would not be foolish enough to permit any open telephone lines into the hangar.

Was there any chance of his climbing over the fence and making his way to the hangar through the abandoned barracks? Or by crossing the old airstrip? Neither route seemed feasible. Nor was he certain he had the strength to go that far on foot. The nausea and dizziness was still coming and going.

The only chance was the gate, he decided; a direct frontal attack that might find someone in the Air Force not quite as efficient as he was supposed to be.

He turned on the car's interior light and checked his forehead in the mirror. The inch-long gash was on the right side, just under the hairline. He wiped the blood away with a handkerchief and combed his hair with his fingers. Then he stepped out of the car and brushed the dirt off his jacket and pants. He was ready.

The guard stepped out of the office as Steve approached, his automatic rifle poised across his waist. He was a slender kid of about twenty, a lock of dark hair visible under his white helmet. Steve had his NASA identification card ready. He stopped in front of the gate arm and handed it over. "Evening, Corporal."

"Evening, sir," the kid said with a strong southern accent. He looked at the card and back at Steve. He glanced into the back seat, then moved back toward the office. "Be just a minute, sir."

"What you'd better do, Corporal, is call Harry Forbes at Hangar 18. He's expecting me."

The kid hesitated and glanced at the card again. "I gotta call Major Franks' office, sir." He picked up the phone.

"Well, Major Franks may not have heard I'm coming. Mr. Forbes called me about a half hour ago. It's kind of an emergency. You'd better check directly with him."

"Can't do that, sir. Ain't no direct lines into Hangar 18."

Steve's heart sank. "Well, have Major Franks talk to Mr. Forbes."

The kid nodded and spoke softly into the phone. He nodded, looked over at Steve and then turned half away, reading something from the NASA card. He finally hung up and came back to the car. "Be a couple minutes, sir. They're checkin'."

"You from Alabama?" Steve asked.

"Macon, sir. Georgia."

"Oh? I've spent a lot of time next door in Florida. Cape Canaveral."

The kid wasn't interested. "That so?" he said dully. He turned and looked into the base, as if expecting to see someone coming. Harry Forbes, maybe? Steve couldn't believe his luck would be that good.

Over to the right and just inside the fence, he suddenly noticed a jeep parked in the shadows. Leaning against the side, two white-helmeted men were smoking, talking casually. *Damn*, he thought. If he had to make a run for it, he was hoping he would have only the corporal to deal with.

Whoever the corporal was waiting for finally appeared. A pair of headlights came over the crest of the hill, directly in front of them, traveling fairly fast. God, let it be Harry, Steve thought.

A half a block away, the car slowed down, then

rolled to a stop a hundred feet from the gate. Two men got out of the front seat and came striding forward.

Steve didn't wait for introductions. He had seen the men's twin brothers less than an hour ago. And before that in Bannon County, Arizona. They had the same dark suits, the same striped ties, and the same coldly impassive faces. Before they were three paces from their car, he dropped the gear lever into "drive" and shoved the throttle to the floor.

The gate arm snapped off like a toothpick and went skittering across the road. The two men froze for an instant, locked in the beam of Steve's headlight. Then they dove desperately to the sides. An instant later they were gone behind him, and Steve was racing up the narrow road at full speed. Racing around an army base full of soldiers seemed hopeless. But he had no other choice now. When he reached the crest of the hill, he glanced in the mirror and saw two pairs of headlights swing around and start after him.

There were several roads going off to the right. The first one led into the barracks area. He passed that and swung into the second, skidding, taking the corner much too fast. Easy, he told himself as he got the car straightened and headed down the slope. The last thing he needed now was an accident.

Which one was Hangar 18? Several buildings had floodlights around them. It had to be the biggest one. It was about a block to the left, a huge corrugated iron building towering a full thirty feet above the others. When he was approximately even with it, he turned left between two dark buildings. Then his heart stopped.

Coming directly at him were two pairs of headlights, each with a red light above them. At the end of the building he turned sharply to the right, then quickly left again, through an open hangar. Tools, or pieces of junk, were scattered over the floor. They clattered under the car and went flying.

At the other end of the hangar, he turned left, then right again. He had no idea where he was now.

He swung the wheel hard into the open door of a second hangar. An instant later, heavy drums and planks were crashing down on him from all sides, and the car came to an abrupt halt. He shoved the gear lever into reverse and gunned the engine. Nothing happened. One of his rear wheels apparently was lifted off the ground, spinning freely. He quickly pushed open the door and ran.

He crossed an alleyway and ducked behind a pile of crates as a jeep came swinging around the corner two buildings down.

It passed by quickly and disappeared around a corner.

He moved out of the shadows and followed the wall of the building, suddenly feeling dizzy again. He couldn't go on much farther, he told himself. His head was pounding so hard he could hardly keep his eyes open. His hand struck something as it brushed along the wall. A doorknob. He turned it and the door opened.

It seemed to be a utility room of some kind. There was a workbench with tools. And shovels and rakes were stacked in a corner. Gasping for breath, Steve eased himself to the floor and crawled under the bench. He propped his back against the wall, then rested his head on his knees. He breathed deeply, fighting to stay conscious.

Lafferty was waiting in the park. He was standing next to his car, his hands in his pockets, looking bored. As quickly as Cain's Cadillac slid into the curb and the headlights went off, he strolled to the back door and let himself in. There was no greeting this time. Lafferty slammed the door, looked at Cain and waited.

The man was completely bloodless, Cain decided. He was a programmed machine that neither laughed nor cried, nor cared about anything.

Cain took a deep breath and sighed. "Price is dead. The other one, Bancroft, is still running around

Texas somewhere, and now Forbes is threatening to blow everything wide open. Is that why you asked me to stay near a phone?"

There was no movement, but Lafferty seemed to shrug. "There are always risks. You knew that."

"We were talking about saving the president from an embarrassment. But there's far more potential damage here than just an election. A lot of people could be implicated."

Lafferty gave him that quarter-inch nod again. "Is there something productive we could discuss? Or did you ask me here to hold your hand while you fret about your problem?"

"It's your problem, too, Mr. Lafferty."

The head moved sideways this time. "I don't have problems. I'm very good at my business." He sighed wearily. "There are always choices, Mr. Cain. Not always pleasant choices. But choices nonetheless. Now, you can let the problem continue to depress you. Or, . . . you can endorse a solution."

Cain stared at the impassive face, knowing the choice would be unacceptable, and that he would have to accept it. "Go on."

"Eliminate Hangar 18."

"What do you mean, eliminate it? There are twenty or thirty people working in that hangar. Are you suggesting . . . ?"

Lafferty's silence expressed very eloquently what he was suggesting. The solution was what the CIA people called "maximum demotion." Or "Tweep"—termination with extreme prejudice. Or any one of a dozen other euphemisms meaning murder.

Cain was surprised to find that he was not shocked. It was a shocking proposal, but for some reason, sitting in the park in the warm comfort of his Cadillac, it was nothing more than words. He dropped back in the seat and gazed out at the shadowy forms of trees and bushes in the park.

If Duncan Tyler did not win a second term, Gordon Cain would be nothing. His name would always have the word "former" in front of it, and he would be back in a suburban California ranch house writing memoirs nobody but his enemies would read.

"On something like this," he said quietly, "we should talk about price."

In the conference room at Hangar 18, Harry and Neal Kelso could hardly believe what they were reading on the computer printout sheets. And the more they read, the more incredible it seemed.

Twenty minutes earlier, Kelso had finally hit on a solution and worked out a matrix for translating the alien writings. Since then, with the aid of three technicians and all the available computers he could find, the translations had been pouring out of the machines at full speed.

"The translation is not perfect," Kelso said as Sarah and Paul Bannister came into the room. He pushed a sheaf of printouts across the table for them. "There are words I couldn't get, and with others the meaning is somewhat vague. But in most cases, I think the general interpretation is accurate."

Sarah was already looking over one of the sheets. "I don't understand," she said and frowned at Harry. "What is this?"

At that moment, Phil Cameron came in and took a seat. Kelso pushed another sheaf of material across to him.

Harry hardly knew where to start. If they learned nothing more from the spacecraft than what Neal Kelso had already translated from the one "library book," they had still made the most profound discovery in the history of the world. It told more about man's origins and evolution than all the history and anthropology books ever written.

"Before any of you start reading," he said, "let me warn you—you're going to find a lot of this unbelievable. So let me tell you where it comes from.

"In what seems like some kind of a library in the spacecraft, Neal found several hundred cubicles containing booklike materials. On one of these were markings that he identified as a symbol designating earth. Since then he has been working on the text of that book. It appears to be some kind of a chronicle, . . . or a sort of recapitulation of the aliens' previous contacts with earth. So that's what we have here.

"As Neal said, the translation is very rough and incomplete. But if what we can read so far is true—and there's no reason to believe it isn't—all the conventional wisdom about the origin of the human race is false."

Both Sarah and Paul Bannister looked up sharply. "What?" Sarah exclaimed.

Harry nodded. "It's a theory we've heard before. Popular books have speculated about it. They titillated the public. But scientists laughed at them. The whole idea was preposterous, they claimed. Fiction. Science fiction. There was no truth to it."

"No truth to what?" Bannister asked.

"All of this," Harry said, nodding at the printouts, "is a report of a previous visit of these men to earth. The dates are obscure, but it must have taken place tens of thousands of years ago."

"Are you serious?" Sarah asked. Both she and Bannister frowned doubtfully at the papers.

"Where did they come from?" Cameron asked.

"That's not clear," Neal Kelso said. "But the book mentions a great pyramid. The description fits the Pyramid of Tetanapa."

"They built it?" Bannister asked.

Kelso nodded. "Apparently."

"As a fortress, most likely," Harry said. "The spacemen were an army on the move. One gets the feeling they were the Roman Legion of their time. But they didn't come to conquer earth. There were no people—people in the sense that we use the word—capable of offering any resistance."

"Then what did they want here?" Sarah asked.

"Evidently they used it as a base."

"And they were here, off and on, for several hundreds of years," Kelso added.

Phil Cameron was shaking his head. "It seems incredible."

"Yes, it does," Harry agreed. "But there's more, Phil. They also speak of the capture, taming, and use of 'animals' as slaves—both male and female. Slaves who worshipped them as gods."

"Tens of thousands of years ago?"

"Yes," Harry said.

"What kinds of animals?" Cameron asked.

"They talked about 'domestic' animals," Kelso said. "At first, I thought they meant something like dogs or cats. But then, when the full translations started coming through, there was a fairly complete description. They were bipeds with opposable thumbs. No tails . . ."

"You mean some kind of pre-humans?" Cameron asked.

Kelso nodded. "Could be."

"And," Harry said, "the report boasts that the females considered it a high honor to live with these gods and to bear their offspring."

"Good Lord," Sarah said softly.

"It's no coincidence that the spacemen are identical to us," Harry said. "It's not a case of two species evolving independently of one another."

Paul Bannister had been scratching his beard, frowning from the printout sheets to Harry and Neal Kelso. "Do you know what you're saying?" he finally exclaimed.

"I'm telling you what we've read, Paul. Those ancient spacemen changed the course of our evolution." Harry hesitated, knowing the reaction he was going to get with his next statement. "They were the 'missing link.' "

Paul Bannister came abruptly to his feet. "Oh, come on!"

"Do you mean to say," Phil Cameron asked, "that these people . . . these aliens, came here tens of thousands of years ago, and that they bred with some kind of sub-human species, who were our ancestors?"

"Yes. But you have to consider both of them our ancestors—the sub-human species, *and* the aliens. We are the descendants of both of them. By breeding with the sub-humans, the aliens raised them to a higher form of life—humans."

"You mean those guys are our grandfathers, so to speak?"

"Yes. Or more accurately, we both had the same grandfathers. However, our grandmothers were the sub-humans."

Paul Bannister was shaking his head. "It's preposterous!"

"It's all in here," Harry said, tapping the printouts. "Read it. Nobody could make up something like this. There are descriptions of dozens of places you'll recognize: the Mediterrenean Sea . . . the Greek Islands . . . the Gulf of Mexico . . . There are even some notes that seem to be about the lost continent of Atlantis. If Neal can fill in some of the blank spaces, we might find out if it really existed and where it was located."

Bannister shook his head. "It's mind-boggling. I still don't believe it."

"Do you believe that spaceship out there?" Harry asked.

"Yes, but . . ."

"It's not a fraud? Or a mirage?"

"No," Bannister admitted.

"Then if you believe that, you have to believe this."

Bannister stared at him for a minute, unable to dispute the logic. He eased back in his chair and picked up one of the printout sheets.

"Listen to this," Cameron said, reading, " 'Ice masses at each axis, one of them considerably larger than the other.' "

"The north and south poles," Kelso said.

" 'Urgent departure for *blank* was ordered,' " Sarah read. " 'It was forbidden to take any of the domesticated animals.' "

"They were probably going to another planet, or another galaxy," Kelso explained. "If I could figure out what that word refers to, and get some kind of a fix on their calendar system, we could learn a lot more about their travels."

Bannister was shaking his head, reading quickly through the sheets. "Incredible," he said softly. "Do you realize what a wealth of information this is? For historians . . . anthropologists . . . geologists . . . Did you say there are hundreds of these 'books' in there?"

"About two hundred and fifty," Kelso said. "Apparently the others deal with different planets, different galaxies . . . who knows?"

"In about a week," Harry said, "we should get permission to open this thing up and get a lot of help in here. Maybe even sooner," he added, thinking about Steve Bancroft. If General Morrison didn't produce Bancroft pretty quick, there were going to be a million people rushing to west Texas by noon tomorrow.

"With more experts and more computers, we can probably get an accurate translation of all those hundreds of books in there. What we find out might be even more mind-boggling than what these printouts have told us. In the field of energy, for example. If we can figure out how that spacecraft operates, it may very well solve all the earth's energy problems. Probably it is some kind of fusion drive, which means they know how to handle nuclear power efficiently and safely. In medicine . . . space travel . . . communications . . . every scientific field imaginable. This could lead to the greatest leap forward in the history of the world." Harry smiled. "So maybe waiting for another week isn't such a tragedy after all."

They all nodded agreement, and Sarah and Paul went back to reading the printouts.

"Neal," Cameron said, "there are some tapes up on the flight deck, too. Maybe you can translate some of the symbols on them."

"Sure," Kelso said. "Let's try it right now."

XIV

Three miles west of Austin, Texas, Lyle Christiansen slowed his truck down and squinted hard through the windshield, searching for a road sign. He finally spotted it on the left—a small, arrow-shaped sign that said *Henley Airport 1 mile*. He checked his mirrors carefully, then swung the truck onto the narrow road.

He downshifted and gunned the engine, giving the throttle just enough pressure to bring his speed back up to twenty-five. Then he carefully scanned the road ahead, watching for potholes.

Lyle had been eating dinner when Mr. Edwards called him. There was a rush delivery, ten cases of nitroglycerine for somebody out at Henley Airport. Lyle didn't mind. He would get time and a half, and he could use the money. He'd hurried down to the plant, and Mr. Edwards was already there to help him load.

Lyle enjoyed driving the truck. There were risks, of course. But he was making twice what any other guys his age were making. And with a wife and two babies, the extra money came in handy. And there was a certain feeling of importance driving down the street in a truck that said DANGER—HIGH EXPLOSIVES on all sides of it.

The men would be waiting by the gate down by the south end, Mr. Edwards had told him. When he reached the little terminal building, Lyle eased his speed down to fifteen and crawled on past, following the fence. Then he saw them, two men in business suits standing in the dark. Lyle edged the truck around the car and stopped in front of the closed gate.

"That'll be fine," one of the men said, coming around to the cab. "We'll carry it in from here."

"Where you takin' it?" Lyle asked.

"Just over to that plane."

About two hundred feet inside the fence, a sleek little Lear Jet was parked next to a black van. Two or three men were moving back and forth to the plane. The van had a big antennae of some kind on the roof.

Lyle grinned.

"Well, I'll tell you, mister. I wouldn't recommend your hand-carryin' this stuff that far. One of you trips on somethin', they'll be pickin' up what's left of you with tweezers."

The two men talked to each other for a minute. Then the short one asked: "You mind if we drive the truck in?"

Lyle shrugged. "Be my guest." He dropped out of the cab and showed the man how the gear-shift operated. "You got an oil blow-out somewheres?" he asked.

The tall man smiled. "Right. Mexico. Down off the gulf coast."

Lyle watched from the gate while the men drove slowly across to the Lear Jet. They backed the truck up to the door, and another man climbed in the plane to help them load the nitro. They were even more careful with the cases than he would have been. Lyle chuckled to himself and lighted a cigarette.

When they finished, the short man drove the truck back to the gate. "There you are, son. Be sure and tell Mr. Edwards thanks."

Lyle drove the truck a short distance toward the terminal building, then doused the lights and pulled in close to the fence. From here he had a better view through the open door of the jet, and he watched curiously, wondering what the two men were up to. It looked like they were fiddling with the tops of the nitro cans, attaching wires to them or something. Maybe some kind of grounding wires so the static electricity wouldn't blow them up by mistake.

When they were done, the two men jumped out and hurriedly closed the door. Then they crossed to the van and disappeared inside. A minute later the jet's engines started humming.

Strange. As far as Lyle could see there wasn't anybody inside the jet. At least he couldn't see anybody up in the cockpit. Lyle slid quietly out of the truck and moved closer to the fence. The jet was moving now, taxiing slowly past Lyle, heading for the end of the runway. And the cockpit was empty!

It didn't even hesitate when it got down to the far end of the field. It just made a broad turn, picking up speed all the time, and then it was racing along the runway, the engines screaming. Five seconds later, the nose lifted and it was going up like a bullet, making a broad turn toward the north.

Lyle shook his head and moved back to the truck. It was the damndest thing he had ever seen. Smart though, when you were carrying nitro. Except those men didn't seem to realize that Mexico was to the south—not to the north.

From the inside of the dark utility room, Steve Bancroft edged the door open a half inch and peered out. In the past five minutes he had heard two jeeps go by. And then someone had hurried past on foot, shouting instructions to someone farther up the road. But now the area seemed to be quiet.

His head was still throbbing, but the nausea had subsided. For the moment his vision seemed to be normal again. How long had he been unconscious? he wondered. Thirty minutes? An hour?

The windows were all dark in the building across from him. Fifty yards to the right, he could see the glow of floodlights reflecting in the sky, and he could hear the intermittent crackle of voices on the jeep radios. The hangar had to be down there somewhere. He moved through the door, closed it quietly behind him and stood in the shadows for a minute. On the workbench in the utility room he had found a heavy pipe wrench. He hefted it in his right hand, then loped quickly across to the other building. Staying close to the wall, he followed the length of it down the slope to the corner, then quickly ducked back into the shadows.

A jeep was coming, cruising slowly, playing a spotlight back and forth across the buildings. Steve flattened himself in the tall grass next to the wall. The spotlight swept over him, and the jeep idled past. When it was gone, he pulled himself up and ran.

He passed two more buildings, turned right and followed another one to the end. About a block away, two jeeps were stopped in the roadway, the drivers talking to each other. Steve loped across to the next building and pressed himself into the shadows. He peered back toward the jeeps, then cursed softly. The one facing him was moving, coming toward him. Had the driver seen him? He moved quickly to a door and ducked inside.

It was a small room with a dusty desk and five or six crates stacked in a corner. In the inner wall was another door with a faint line of light showing beneath it. He stared uneasily at the door, then turned and listened for the jeep, the pipe wrench ready.

A full minute passed and he heard nothing. The jeep must have stopped, or turned a corner and gone in a different direction. He eased the wrench down. Then he caught his breath and quickly turned, the wrench hoisted again.

There were footsteps coming toward the inner door. A moment later, the knob turned and the door swung open. In the harsh light from the hallway, Steve could see only the outline of a man. He lifted the wrench higher and moved forward.

"Steve!"

He froze, the wrench still poised to strike. He still couldn't see the man's face. "Harry?"

Then the lights came on and Harry Forbes was gaping at him, his hand still on the light switch. "Are you all right?"

Steve felt like the whole upside down world had finally righted itself. He lowered the wrench and sagged against the old desk. "God, am I glad to see you, Harry. What are you doing here?"

"The base security office called. They said you were running around the base somewhere."

Steve's heart jumped again. "Base security?"

Harry frowned at him. "What happened to your head?"

He had forgotten about his headache and the welt on his forehead. "Harry . . . Lew is dead."

"I know. I heard about it on the radio. Come on." Harry reached for his elbow.

"Where to?" Steve asked suspiciously.

"This is Hangar 18. You're safe here. Come on."

Steve moved through the door as Harry switched off the light. "The UFO . . . is it . . . ?"

"It's here."

Harry pushed open another door and suddenly they were in a cavernous, brightly lit hangar. Steve squinted against the lights for a minute. Then he saw it, the glistening black form of the spacecraft. He stared numbly at it, feeling nothing.

It was an ugly thing—a raised platform with what looked like a cluster of crude boilers sitting on top. It was to keep them from seeing this that he and Lew had been chased all over the country. And it was for this Lew had been killed. "There it is," he said dully. "They didn't want us to talk about it, and there it is."

He turned sharply to Harry, the anger and frustration suddenly flaring inside him again. "Harry, they killed Lew! They tried to kill me. We've been set up from the start. What's going on?!"

Harry shook his head. "I'm not sure."

159

"They've been chasing us all over the country, Harry. And there's two of them right here on this base! They tried to stop me from coming in!"

Harry stared at him, feeling a little sick. From the moment he had switched on the light in that dusty office, he knew all his suspicions about General Morrison were true. Morrison had lied to him from the beginning—about Steve and Lew . . . about "orders from the White House" . . . probably about what had happened to the girl they had found in the spacecraft. And now Lew Price was dead.

No matter what excuses Morrison gave him now, there was going to be a press conference tomorrow morning. The whole world was going to know what was in Hangar 18. And they were also going to know what happened to Lew Price. Harry turned abruptly for the door. "Come on into my office. I want you to tell me everything that's happened. Then I'm going to get some answers." He pulled the door open for Steve.

"Answers from who?"

"From General Frank Morrison."

On the flight deck of the spacecraft, Phil Cameron punched the button, starting the "Earth" tape going for the third time. The symbol came on and faded. Then the series of short clips began again: the power plants . . . missile silos . . . defense installations . . . the big cities of the world—all overlaid with the grid patterns.

Neal Kelso had already watched the tape once. Then he had brought in a computer terminal and started feeding in the symbols that appeared at the bottom of each picture. For fifteen minutes now he had been working in silence, punching keys, watching his readout screen, then punching more keys.

Earlier, Harry Forbes had commented that it made sense for the aliens to have taken pictures of all those things—compiling a record of how humans lived and how advanced their technology was. But Cameron couldn't help feeling there was more to it than that. Of the thousands of examples of human technology, these pictures were limited solely to military and nuclear installations, along with shots of big cities. He could understand their interest in our weapons and defense installations. But why were such pictures on the same tape as the pictures of the cities?

"Phil . . . ?" Neal Kelso suddenly said. He was still frowning at his computer screen, but he had stopped punching buttons. He looked up, his frown darker than ever. "Phil, . . . I think these are *targets!*" He looked at the big screen in front of Cameron where a picture of the Strategic Air Command headquarters was just fading away. "They're all *targets!*"

Cameron stared at him. "Targets? What do you mean, targets?"

"They're all designated landing zones for alien spacecrafts! On every picture there are specific instructions detailing the safest and the most strategically advantageous place for a spacecraft to land."

Cameron looked from Kelso to the big screen. "You mean they're going to attack these places?"

"I don't know. But the grid patterns are navigational directions for the landings. And at each of the nuclear power plants, and at each of the missile silos, the small notations on the left are about the presence of fissionable material. The pictures with cities don't have those."

Cameron stared at the screen again seeing a close-up shot of the San Onofre nuclear power plant on the coast of California. A few seconds later the power plant was replaced by a picture of March Air Force Base, about sixty miles east of the power plant. On the flat, desert-like terrain, the drooping wings of five B-52 bombers were clearly distinguishable on the far side of the runway.

"See the characters on the bottom left," Kelso said. "Those are the notations about fissionable material."

Cameron nodded uneasily. "The B-52's carry nuclear bombs for SAC."

The picture changed, this time showing what looked like Norton Air Force Base, a few miles north of March. "When?" Cameron asked.

Kelso frowned at him.

"*When* are the spacecrafts scheduled to land?"

Kelso shook his head. "Maybe the characters on the right side of the pictures . . ." He consulted his matrix and started punching keys on the computer again.

Cameron felt his heart thudding faster as he watched more pictures come on the screen. It made sense. If someone wanted to take over the world and forestall any defensive measures, the first thing they would try to do was capture or destroy all nuclear materials.

Did it mean they had no fear of conventional weapons? Considering the ray-gun on this spacecraft—and the fact that the spacecraft had suffered no apparent damage from being enveloped in burning rocket fuel—ordinary weapons probably meant nothing to them.

"Phil . . . ?" Kelso was staring at him again, his face white. "The other symbols are dates and times. Very precise dates and times."

Cameron moved quickly to his side and looked at the computer screen as Kelso pushed more buttons.

A garbled sequence of numbers and letters changed so rapidly they were incomprehensible. Then the flashing stopped and three sets of words and numbers fixed themselves on the screen. They were specific dates and times—down to the minutes and seconds. "Oh, my God," Cameron breathed.

Kelso opened his mouth and closed it again. Then he looked up at Cameron. "We've got to tell Harry!"

Cameron grabbed his walkie-talkie from where he had left it by the controls. "Harry!" he called. He re-

leased the "transmit" button, but there was no answer.
"Harry!" he called again. Then he frowned at Kelso.

Kelso had been punching more computer keys.
But then he had suddenly stopped. Now he was gaping
at the big screen over the spacecraft controls. Cameron
turned and looked.

The pictures were still coming on and fading
away. But the characters at the bottom were now disappearing. As quickly as a new picture came on, the
symbols appeared for a moment. Then they broke up
and disappeared. It was as if somebody was erasing
them.

"Phil . . . look!"

Kelso was pointing at one of the control panels.
Buttons were being depressed with nobody touching
them. Above the panel, lights were coming on and off.
The movement of the buttons seemed to be synchro-
nized with the disappearance of the characters from the
pictures.

Cameron quickly moved across and pushed the
button that normally would have stopped the pictures
on the screen. This time nothing happened. The pictures continued fading in and out, the characters at the
bottom being erased as quickly as the pictures appeared. Cameron touched other buttons—those that he
had experimented with earlier. Now they all seemed to
be locked in place. It was as if all the control mecha-
nisms in the spacecraft had been taken over by some
outside force.

"Good God," Cameron breathed. The spacecraft
was being monitored from somewhere. He and Harry
had speculated about the possibility earlier. But neither
of them had taken it too seriously. It was apparent now
that their speculations had been correct. Somebody,
somewhere, was watching and listening to everything
they did. And now that Kelso had worked out the
translations, everything was being erased! Cameron
switched on his walkie-talkie again. "Harry!" he
shouted. There was still no answer.

As if hypnotized, Kelso was still gaping at the buttons and the blinking lights on the control panel. The buttons were still clicking on and off, and the characters were steadily disappearing.

"Come on," Cameron said. "We've got to find Harry!"

Kelso looked up, then pulled himself from the chair and followed Cameron to the elevator.

My God, Cameron thought as they crossed the lower chamber and headed down the ramp, they had to contact SAC immediately, and the president.

Neither one of them was conscious of the faint whine coming from somewhere high above the hangar. At that moment the sound was barely distinguishable from the normal hum of testing equipment surrounding the spacecraft.

Sarah Michaels and Paul Bannister had taken several sheafs of computer printouts to the small coffee room next to the hospital. On the couch, Bannister glanced up from his reading and frowned, listening to the rising scream. At first he thought it might be coming from something in the hangar. Then he realized that it was nothing more than a jet airplane.

He turned his attention back to the printouts and lightly scratched his beard as he continued reading. He believed it now. The whole thing was incredible. But the evidence was too overwhelming to deny. He felt like someone living in the dark ages who had suddenly come upon a twentieth century history book.

In the conference room, Harry had called General Morrison's home, but nobody answered. Then he had tried the Pentagon where the operator told him Morrison was attending a dinner party at General Curry's house. But Morrison was not there. Finally he had asked the Pentagon operator to try Morrison's office, and the General's weary voice came on after the fifth ring.

"Hold on a minute," Harry said and covered the mouthpiece. A jet airplane was coming in over the hangar—its engines screaming so loud Harry couldn't hear a thing.

In Harry's office, Steve Bancroft was gazing silently through the window at the alien spacecraft, still angered by the events of the past two days. Lew Price had been certain the UFO was hidden in Hangar 18. If only he had lived long enough to see the thing.

Steve watched Phil Cameron and a bearded man come out of the spacecraft and hurry across the hangar to the offices. Then he lifted his head and squinted at the ceiling of the hangar. It sounded like a jet was coming in for a landing. But it was awfully low, and it was coming much too fast for a landing approach.

Lt. Giles from Saginaw, Michigan, was standing by the front gate when he first noticed the plane. It must have been at five or six thousand feet then, coming down in an almost vertical dive. Some hot-rock fighter pilot who was going to buzz the hangar area and pull up at the last second.

He watched the plane, and then his heart stopped. There was no chance of it pulling up, he realized. It was less than five hundred feet from the ground and still in a vertical dive. A split second later a huge mushroom of fire erupted from the hangar area beyond the barracks. Then the thunderous explosion almost knocked him from his feet.

"Holy Christ!" the corporal shouted, and came bolting out of the office. Lt. Giles ran for his jeep.

Two minutes later he skidded to a stop on the hill overlooking the hangar, his mouth agape.

There was no point in hurrying down there. Hangar 18 was gone. There wasn't even much burning around it. The whole area was a smoldering empty space, with only a few flames coming from the pieces of debris that had been scattered out on the runway. About the only thing left was a funny looking black thing with flashing lights sitting in the middle of where the hangar used to be.

ABOUT THE AUTHOR

ROBERT WEVERKA was born in Los Angeles and educated at the University of Southern California, where he majored in economics. His other novels include: *Griff, Search, The Sting, Moonrock, The Widowed Master, One Minute to Eternity, Apple's Way, The Waltons, I Love My Wife, March or Die, Avalanche* and *The Magic of Lassie.* He and his family currently live in Idyllwild, California.

CHARLES E. SELLIER, JR. performs the multiple duties of executive, producer, and writer for one of the most active and successful production and distribution companies in today's film industry. As President, both for the Production Company, Schick Sunn Classic Productions, and its distribution subsidiary company, Sunn Classic Pictures, Sellier restricts his productions only to films suitable for the family viewing audience.

Sellier has authored such books as *The Lincoln Conspiracy, The Life and Times of Grizzly Adams,* and *In Search of Noah's Ark*—all were followed by successful film productions produced by him. In his 19 year filmmaking career, he has also produced many other theatrical films including *Beyond and Back, The Brothers O'Toole, The Bermuda Triangle, The Fall of the House of Usher, Mountainman, The Outer Space Connection, The Mysterious Monsters,* and *In Search of Historic Jesus.*

Dividing his writing and theatrical film production activities with television programming production, Sellier, with typical enthusiasm, created and produced the Classics Illustrated series of two hour special films for N.B.C. which included the classic stories, *The Last of the Mohicans, The Time Machine, The Deerslayer,* and *The Incredible Rocky Mountain Race.* He has also produced and created the popular *Grizzly Adams, Mark Twain's America,* and *Greatest Heroes of the Bible* series.

Sellier makes his home in the historic silver mining town and now renowned skiing area of Park City, Utah in the rugged Wasatch mountain range.

RELAX!
SIT DOWN
and Catch Up On Your Reading!

☐	13098	THE MATARESE CIRCLE by Robert Ludlum	$3.50
☐	12206	THE HOLCROFT COVENANT by Robert Ludlum	$2.75
☐	13688	TRINITY by Leon Uris	$3.50
☐	13899	THE MEDITERRANEAN CAPER by Clive Cussler	$2.75
☐	13396	THE ISLAND by Peter Benchley	$2.75
☐	12152	DAYS OF WINTER by Cynthia Freeman	$2.50
☐	13201	PROTEUS by Morris West	$2.75
☐	13028	OVERLOAD by Arthur Hailey	$2.95
☐	13220	A MURDER OF QUALITY by John Le Carre	$2.25
☐	11745	THE HONOURABLE SCHOOLBOY by John Le Carre	$2.75
☐	13471	THE ROSARY MURDERS by William Kienzle	$2.50
☐	13848	THE EAGLE HAS LANDED Jack Higgins	$2.75
☐	13880	RAISE THE TITANIC! by Clive Cussler	$2.75
☐	13186	THE LOVE MACHINE by Jacqueline Susann	$2.50
☐	12941	DRAGONARD by Rupert Gilchrist	$2.25
☐	14463	ICEBERG by Clive Cussler	$2.75
☐	12810	VIXEN 03 by Clive Cussler	$2.75
☐	14033	ICE! by Arnold Federbush	$2.50
☐	11820	FIREFOX by Craig Thomas	$2.50
☐	12691	WOLFSBANE by Craig Thomas	$2.50
☐	13896	THE ODESSA FILE by Frederick Forsyth	$2.75

Buy them at your local bookstore or use this handy coupon for ordering